Tempered Truth

Pamela S. Thibodeaux

And you shall know the truth and the truth shall set you free. ~ John 8:32

TEMPERED TRUTH

Book 5 in the Tempered Series

By Pamela S Thibodeaux

Publisher/Distributor:

Temperance Publishing; an imprint of

Pamela S. Thibodeaux Enterprises, LLC

PO Box 324 Iowa, LA 70647

Copyright © 2021 by Pamela S. Thibodeaux

ISBN# 978-1-7353393-0-6

Cover Design: Delia Latham (Heaven's Touch Designs)

Published in the Unites States of America

Publishing History: First edition March 15th, 2021

Dedication

To my faithful Tempered fans new and old. Thank you for following this series from beginning to end. I pray you are blessed 100-fold for your continued love and support. I appreciate you more than words can say!

If you enjoy **Tempered Truth**, please write a positive review and post it at online retailers (Amazon, B&N, Kobo, iBooks, etc.) and websites where readers gather and/or your social media platforms (FaceBook, Good Reads, BookBub, Twitter, etc).

Sign up to receive my **Newsletter** (http://bit.ly/psthibnewsletter) and get a FREE short story.

Praise for Pamela S. Thibodeaux

"Pamela Thibodeaux uses her masterful story writing art to create a powerful story of how God heals a woman's heart —broken by grief— through recovery, love and triumph." ~ CBA Best-Selling Author DiAnn Mills on **My Heart Weeps**.

"A great collection of short stories. Each one includes inspirational romance. Wonderful choice when you need a quick pick-me-up. I have not been one to read short stories. This book has changed that. There are times when they are the perfect choice." ~ (Amazon) Review of **Love in Season** by K. Neely

"Loved this book. Wish everyone could read this. Definitely puts all holidays in perspective. If we remember the reason for the holidays then we must put God first.......always. I will certainly recommend this book. Great stuff keep up the great writing." ~ (Amazon) Review of **Keri's Christmas Wish** by Reba

"Oh, the passion, faith and just LIFE that flows through this book...powerful writing indeed!" ~ Review

of **Circles of Fate** by Deena Peterson, Book Reviewer @ A Peek at my Bookshelf and Just One More

"Thibodeaux leads the reader through from the first page to the last without once relinquishing control. She hooks them, holds them, and keeps them enthralled until the last line." ~ Review of **The Visionary** by Delia Latham, author of the "Solomon's Gate" series

"In His Sight caught my attention from the beginning and it made me wonder if I had given all to God as he gave all to me. Thank you, Pamela, for a story that I would readily recommend to anyone who needs that extra encouragement!" ~ Reviewed by Wendy for Happily Ever After Reviews *Part of **Love in Season** collection of short stories*

"Winter Madness is a wonderful romance and an excellent example of Spiritual growth." ~Reviewed by Dee Daily for The Romance Studio *Part of **Love in Season** collection of short stories*

"***A Hero for Jessica*** is a good, sweet read charged with attraction but an emphasis on true love. I recommend it to women of all ages." ~ Reviewed by Violet for LASR *Part of ***Love in Season*** collection of short stories*

"***Cathy's Angel*** is a short tale that is entertaining as well as inspiring. Well done!" ~ Reviewed by Marlene for Fallen Angel Reviews *Part of ***Love in Season*** collection of short stories*

"Pamela S. Thibodeaux's motto is "Inspirational with an Edge! ™" Her short story ***Choices*** lives up to those words and is well worth reading." ~ Reviewed by Gail for Night Owl Romance *Part of ***Love in Season*** collection of short stories*

"***The Inheritance*** was my first Thibodeaux work; however, it will not be my last! Her approach to writing about everyday life, while struggling to maintain strict Christian standards and values, is a glimpse into reality which we all must face from time to time." ~ Reviewed by Brenda Talley for The Romance Studio

"If you have ever considered Christian fiction bland, then check out the **Tempered Series.** It will be well worth your time." ~ Amanda Killgore for Huntress Reviews

"***Lori's Redemption*** is fast paced, lots of action, gripping storyline... I loved it. It's gone straight back into my TBR pile." ~ Clare Revell author of the "Monday's Child" series

"Through Pamela's blessed ability to find God everywhere, even in secular song lyrics, she has written devotions guaranteed to touch the heart and remind the reader of our True Love, the Rose of Sharon." ~ Endorsement for ***Love is a Rose*** by Linda Yezak, Author, Editor Triple Edge Critique Service

Tempered Truth

Pamela S. Thibodeaux

And you shall know the truth and the truth shall set you free. ~ John 8:32

Prologue

September 18, 2001

Scott Hensley sat in the den of his Louisiana home, his heart heavy, overwhelmed with the same sense of shock and grief that rocked the nation. Upstairs, his wife, Katrina, nursed his infant daughter while his sons did homework in their rooms. All normal activities in a world that was far from normal.

One week ago, on a beautiful fall morning much like this one, terrorists waged an attack on America the likes of which he'd never expected to see in his lifetime. Scott sat in frozen horror as the events replayed on the television. He hated seeing the terror and panic over and over yet, found it hard to tear himself away. Since that day, his wife had been in tears, his sons subdued and afraid, their innocence stripped away by an unknown evil. Only his three-month-old daughter remained unaffected.

His adopted daughter Lexie, due to make him a grandfather by year's end, called daily just to hear their voices and to reassure herself–and his friends of a lifetime, the family she had married into–of their wellbeing.

Scott's mind wandered back to another act of terrorism nearly twenty years ago that had changed his life. He'd been on a three-month mission in South America. During his second month there, his family flew down to visit him—his mother and father always so proud, and Melissa, his wife. The memories surfaced as though it happened yesterday...

The airplane rising boldly against a brilliant summer sky...the sound of an explosion...the sight of that ball of fire and black smoke billowing out of the plane as it spiraled toward the earth to crash into a crumbled heap of burning metal and flesh.

The same sense of loss and helpless anger filled him now as it had then. The fact their deaths were still considered a senseless and unsolved act of terrorism only added to the grief he'd carried in his heart for so long. That grief surfaced now, with his country and its freedom under attack.

Getting up, he poured a liberal amount of whiskey into a glass, downed it in one gulp and poured another, then strode across the room to turn the television off.

He knocked back the second shot of alcohol then slung the crystal on a surge of impotent fury. A sound, much like that of a wounded or enraged animal, escaped his throat, and he buried his head in shaking hands. How he made it back across the room to collapse on the couch would always remain a mystery.

Conceived in wartime, Scott had never been called upon to defend his country during the conflicts to follow because he had no siblings. However, he'd seen enough carnage in his years as a physician to equal a lifetime of combat.

His mind circled through the years of his life until it rested once more on the matter in his heart that had never been completely settled.

Who was he?

The question had arisen at different points in his life, though Scott had never felt the need to have it answered. He knew who he was: *Dr. Richard Scott Hensley, born of Rosa Sanchez Hensley and Jonathan Scott Hensley, Bandera, Texas, 1944* with roots as deep as the rich Texas soil.

But now, with the country in turmoil, the existence of his children, and his daughter about to give birth to his first grandchild, the answer seemed imperative.

Would he have the courage and strength to withstand whatever the answer turned out to be?

He rose and picked up the miraculously unbroken tumbler. After rinsing it in the kitchen, he returned to the den and poured liquor until it danced at the rim of the crystal jigger. Scott took a sip so it wouldn't spill onto the carpet as he walked to his desk. With shaking hands, he retrieved an envelope that had lain unopened for nearly a quarter of a century. Though faded and yellow, the letter still elicited the same deep-seated fear and panic he'd experienced the day he received it.

Sweat pooled in his palms. His hands trembled. Scott took another taste and walked quickly to the couch before his knees gave way. He tossed the envelope onto the coffee table, set the drink next to it, and raked his hands over his face. The five o'clock shadow scraped his skin. Scott welcomed the contrast, the feeling of something other than excruciating fear.

God, why? *What difference will opening this thing make now?*

The answer came as it usually did, in a well-known, much-loved scripture...

You shall know the truth and the truth shall set you free.

Still, Scott hesitated. Somehow, somewhere deep down inside, he knew once he opened the envelope a part of him would never be the same.

He picked up the drink with one hand and the letter with the other then leaned back into the buttery leather cushions of the couch. *Slap! Slap! Slap!* He beat the envelope against his thigh, drank. His mother's handwriting beckoned. He closed his eyes and saw her face. Smelled her perfume. Felt her touch. Heard her voice...

"I love you, Scott, and I'm so very proud of you."

Before he could change his mind, Scott put down his whiskey, slid his finger beneath the flap to break the seal then ran it along the edge until it lay open in the palm of his hand. Again, he hesitated, while his breath came in sharp, almost painful bursts. His heart thundered in his chest.

Taking a deep breath, he withdrew the pages from their nest, resisting the urge to crumple it up like trash and throw it away. He raised the beaker again and swallowed the remaining contents.

Liquid courage.

Sending a silent plea to God to get him through this, he set the glass down and unfolded the letter. A wave of grief washed over him at the sight of his mother's handwriting, so bold and beautiful. Scott blinked back the tears with determination and read...

My darling son, your father has encouraged me for years to write this letter. The words contained within these pages may bring you anger and pain, perhaps bitterness or shame. Read them anyway and read them often, keeping in mind how very much you are loved and that your life, your very existence—no matter how painful—is worth far more than words can express. It is my prayer that you will end up with a deeper realization and understanding of the healing power of love and the saving grace of our Lord Jesus Christ...

Chapter One

Scott wiped the tears from his cheeks. He was right, had been right all along, in thinking he would not be the same after reading what was inside that envelope. And he wasn't. He was better, richer, wiser. He possessed a deeper understanding of who he was, why he was here, and what love—true, *sacrificial* love, was all about.

As usual, his mind turned to Craig Harris, his friend of a lifetime. He remembered how difficult Craig's childhood had been, how strong he'd become, how close they were, and how blessed he was to have him in his life. Through the love and wisdom God had given his parents, he'd had it all... *a best friend and a brother,* and his life was far richer than it would have been had they not been obedient to Him.

* * *

Three months later, in Craig's home, Scott sat at the kitchen table enjoying the peace and quiet as the house settled down around them. Craig's daughter Amber and her husband Stanley had taken their children home, excitedly anticipating the visit of one jolly old elf.

Upstairs, Scott's wife Trina, nursed his daughter in hopes of getting her settled down for the evening. At barely six months old, Rikki Jayne was fascinated by the sights, sounds, and excitement of Christmas. His sons, Richard, and Robert slept in the den. Scott's adopted daughter Lexie, who was married to Craig's son Ace, had long-since retired for the evening, their infant daughter tucked snugly in her bassinet.

"What a day." Craig sighed, stretched his legs, and wished aloud he were in front of a roaring fire.

Scott nodded. "It's been a full one." How should he broach the subject uppermost in his mind? "You know, Lexie has asked several times how we could go so long without knowing if we were blood relations. I told her that we've never felt the *need* to know and that we were closer than many blood brothers ever were. But, I guess, considering her childhood, she would want to know, especially since becoming a mother herself."

Craig eyed him, a curious lift to his brow. "Are you feeling the need to know?"

Scott thought about his mother's letter. They'd always been brothers at heart. Blood or the lack thereof had never made a difference, wouldn't change things now. He shrugged. "Not really. I've always been happy and satisfied having you as my friend. I truly don't believe anything would ever change that."

"But?" Craig queried, clearly noting the hesitancy in his voice.

Scott sighed; tears filled his eyes. "But the events of September eleventh stirred up old questions. I can't believe it's been over three months. The pain is still so raw."

"Neither can I," Craig said, his voice solemn, then smiled. "But you're right. Nothing will alter the bond we share. Not this late in the game anyway. We're too old and set in our ways to change the way we feel about each other now." He grinned, then sobered. "You've been more than a friend to me these fifty-plus years and I'll always be grateful you are a part of my life."

Not realizing until that moment how much those words truly meant, Scott took a deep breath and smiled. "In that case, how about a drink?" He got up to retrieve a decanter of brandy and two tumblers, then poured.

Craig accepted the drink with a sigh of appreciation and raised it in salute. "To little Tamera Joy. May she grow into the name and grace her parents' lives with joyful misery." He chuckled. "Just as her grandmother graced ours and would expect of her namesake."

Scott laughed and took a sip then raised the jigger again. "I was thinking more along the lines of to you, *my brother*, and to our beautiful granddaughter."

The truth burst to light in Craig's eyes, his smile glowed with warmth. He clinked his glass against Scott's once more. "All right then, for the blessing of family."

They drank and settled back into their chairs. "You want to talk about what you discovered?"

Scott shrugged. "The whys and wherefores don't really matter unless you want to know."

Craig closed his eyes, took a deep breath then shook his head. "Someday, maybe, but not today."

Scott acknowledged the remark with a slight inclination of his head. "That's what I figured, but I want you to know, I've willed my mother's letter to you. Trina knows where to find it."

Craig's gaze cut to him. Questions sharpened the grey eyes that had softened over years of love, loss, grief, and acceptance.

Scott shook his head and grinned. "I don't plan on dying first, or anytime soon," he assured with a chuckle, then grew somber. "But that's something we have no control over." His voice quavered, as did his hand when he lifted the brandy to his lips. "But for the first time in my life I'm.... unsettled....and.... afraid for the safety of myself, my wife, and children. If by some chance God does take me home first, I want you to promise to look after Trina and the kids."

Craig leaned forward and reached over to clasp his shoulder. Scott felt the strength of love and assurance in the simple gesture. Fifty-plus years of friendship passed between them in a look that said it all.

"Goes without saying, buddy."

Relief washed through him like a warm shower. Scott smiled his thanks and lifted his drink once more in salute. Craig sealed the promise with a clink of rims and a final sip.

Chapter Two

February 28th, 2005

Craig settled in for the seven-plus hour drive to Scott's home in Lafayette, Louisiana. His daughter-in-law sat in the back seat so she could take care of his granddaughter should she awaken. Her continued weeping unnerved him. "Lex, please, you've got to get a hold of yourself."

"I don't know what I'm going to do if he dies, Craig. I don't think I can handle it. He's my father. I've already lost one father; I'm not ready to lose Scott too. Oh, God, I can't believe this is happening!"

"We don't yet know how he's doing. Trina said he's stable. Whatever the situation, what he and Trina, need from you now, is your strength and your faith. Besides, being this upset is not healthy for you, especially in your condition. Nor is it good for Tamera Joy."

She sniffled. "You're right. I'm sorry."

He glanced in the rearview mirror and smiled as she rubbed her gently rounded abdomen, then returned his gaze to the road. "No need to apologize. Let's focus on the positive here." *Easier said than done but I hope she can get it together. Neither my heart, nor my nerves, can take much more of her crying.*

Craig swallowed the bitter bile of fear in his throat. Hard to believe barely two months ago he and Scott sat at the kitchen table toasting the holidays, the upcoming New Year, and the joy over their second grandchild.

Now he clung to life in a hospital room.

Lexie's cell phone rang. From her end of the conversation, Craig knew his son was on the line. As she talked to Ace, his gaze remained focused on the road and his heart fixated in prayer.

The hours flew by as quickly as the miles. Stopping only to refuel—the truck and themselves—they drove into the hospital parking lot in record time. Craig disembarked, pocketed his keys, and unbuckled the three-year-old child that was both his and Scott's granddaughter. Lexie brushed her hair, straightened her blouse, and pinched some color into her cheeks.

"Ready?" he asked, lifting Tamera Joy into his arms.

She swallowed hard, nodded, slung Tamera's diaper bag over her shoulder, and exited the vehicle.

"Remember...faith, trust, and strength," Craig encouraged as they made their way inside. Together they presented a united front and hurried to the ICU waiting area.

Trina bolted from her chair and rushed forward to embrace them the moment they walked into the room. Scott's sons lay slumped in chairs across from the one their mother had vacated. Rikki Jayne clamored to her feet in the tiny portable playpen, jabbering in earnest. Her words flowed together in excited gibberish at seeing her sister and niece. A movement caught their eye and the entire family faced Scott's longtime friend and colleague, Dr. Mike Guidry, as he strode through the ICU doors. Crevices of fear, grief, and uncertainty lined his face. Fatigue clouded his eyes.

"How is he?" Craig asked.

Mike heaved a breath. "Right now, he's stable. We've stopped the bleeding, but he's pretty banged up."

"What the hell happened, Mike?"

"A patient in ER went ballistic, slinging a knife around and demanding drugs. Scott got caught in the crossfire along with several others. By the time they got the patient under control, most of the ER staff had cuts and bruises. No one, not even Scott himself, realized how often and how badly he'd been stabbed until he collapsed. They rushed him into surgery and repaired what damage they could. Now all we can do is wait and see."

"Is he awake? Can we see him?"

Trying to respond to both questions at the same

time, Mike resembled a bobble-head doll. "He's unconscious right now, but you can see him. No more than two at a time." He glanced at the boys then back at Trina. "He's not a pretty sight. You might wait until you've seen him before letting the kids go in."

"You can't stop me." Scott's oldest, Richard, spouted the protest, but immediately quieted at a firm look from his mother.

"He can't, but I can." Her tone brooked no argument.

Mike led Trina and Lexie into ICU. After the two had gone, Craig urged Richard back into his seat, then sat next to him. "I know you're worried, but your mother needs your cooperation right now—not attitude."

"He's my father. Lexie's not even blood and she gets to go in."

Craig cringed at the bitterness in the boy's voice. "I can't believe those words came out of your mouth."

"I'm almost fourteen years old and Mom treats me like a baby. He's my father. I want to see him, but you'll probably get to before me."

"Yeah, and at nearly fourteen years old, you should have a little—no...*a lot* more respect for your mother and her feelings." *I know that's asking a lot of any teenager.* Still, he pressed on. "You might be able to pull this attitude with Katrina, but your father wouldn't let you get by with it for long and I think you know that. Neither will I. So, mind yourself, young man, or you'll have no say in whether or not you see anyone or anything but the four walls of your bedroom or your classrooms."

The glare Richard bestowed on him was worthy of an Oscar, but Craig held the boy's gaze until Richard lowered his and mumbled, "Yes, sir."

The two stood when Trina and Lexie came out of ICU, clinging to one another. Craig couldn't tell who was holding up whom. He reached for Trina as she collapsed. Lexie grabbed Richard then drew Robert into their embrace. For several minutes, the only coherent sounds were the broken sobs of the two women.

"Mom." Richard's voice quavered. "I want to see him."

Trina gathered him tight against her chest. Tall like his father, Richard's height made it difficult for her to cuddle him. "Oh baby, you don't want to see him like this. Please, let's give it a day or two."

He jerked away. "I'm not a baby. What if he's not better in a day or two? I can't believe you're keeping me from him."

Trina sank into a chair. Another sob burst from her lips. She buried her face in hands that trembled.

Craig gripped Richard's shoulder, reiterating their earlier conversation with a hard look. When Trina gazed up at him, the devastation in her eyes tore at his heart. "I'll take him with me, if you want."

She turned beseeching eyes toward her son. "I know

you think you're strong and tough, but no child should see his father in this condition."

"I. Am. Not. A. Child." He ground the words between teeth clenched as tightly as the fists by his side. "He's my father. I want to see him, now."

Trina threw up her hands in defeat. "Fine. Don't say I didn't warn you."

Before her younger son could utter a word, she shut him down with one glance and a shake of her head. "You're too young to go in there, Robert. Read the sign— twelve and over."

"But I'm almost twelve," he whined.

"Almost doesn't count. The answer is no. That's final."

Robert flung himself into a chair.

Craig took Richard's arm as they went into the ICU room where Scott lay unconscious, bruised and swollen. Tubes and wires stuck out of him everywhere. Monitors beeped. The harsh sound of the ventilator echoed in the room. Richard sucked in a sharp breath and started to turn around.

Craig clamped a hand on the back of the boy's neck. "Oh, no you don't. Take a good, long look."

He held him in place less than a minute, but long enough to feel the panic emanating from Richard. "Think about this moment the next time you're tempted to buck your mother."

He released his hold and walked to the bedside as Richard fled from the room.

"Oh, God," Craig whispered. He grasped Scott's hand beneath the linens. "I'm here, buddy."

Scott's hand twitched. His eyelids fluttered.

"Don't worry about a thing. I'll be here until you make your way back to us."

When his allotted time was up, Craig returned to the lobby. Over the next several hours he, Lexie, and Trina took turns sitting with Scott.

As the day wore into evening, the boys bickered, the

girls fussed. Wishing for nothing more than a few hours of peace, Craig pushed out of his chair and lifted Trina's chin with his finger. "You need to take Rikki and the boys and go home."

Before she could protest, he turned to Lexie. "You go with her. These babies need to get out of the playpen and into real beds. The boys need a break from here too."

"I want to stay…"

Craig silenced Richard's arguments with a sharp gaze. "I'll call if there is any change."

Lexie picked Tamera Joy up and grabbed her diaper bag. "I'll drive."

Trina handed her the keys to their Suburban without hesitation. She lifted Rikki out of the playpen and handed her to Richard then folded the apparatus. She pushed Rikki's bag into Robert's hands. "I want to see him once more before I go."

Craig carried the playpen out and enlisted the boys'

aide to transfer Tamera Joy's car-seat and Lexie's bags from his truck into the Suburban. Lexie started the vehicle to warm it up and turned to him.

"I can come back."

Craig controlled the urge to roll his eyes and shake her. "You should rest. Trina and the boys need you with them. I'll be fine. Beginning tomorrow we can take shifts or something. We'll work it out later."

Mike escorted Trina through the hospital doors and helped her into the passenger seat. He turned to Craig as Lexie backed out of the parking spot and into the line of vehicles exiting the hospital garage. "I'm glad you convinced Trina to leave. She and those kids have been here too long already."

Craig heaved a sigh and rubbed the back of his neck. "I figured I'd have a fight on my hands, but she didn't argue at all. Which proves how exhausted she is."

Mike nodded his agreement, and the two men made their way back to the ICU lounge.

Chapter Three

Craig awoke with a jolt when 'Code Blue' echoed through the corridors. Squeaky shoes scurried past as doctors and nurses scrambled from all corners of the building. He rose as Mike approached, but before he could hail him, the doctor grabbed a chart and rushed into the Intensive Care unit. He walked toward the double doors only to be stopped by a nurse.

"Sir, you can't go in."

"I want to know how Scott is. Dr. Hensley? How is he?"

"I don't know, but no one is allowed inside while we're in the middle of an emergency. If you'll have a seat, I'll try to find out something on Dr. Hensley."

Craig bit back his impatience and paced while the nurse strode through the doors and disappeared around the corner. He turned on his heel and walked across the hall. An eerie silence permeated the air, broken only by the clatter of his boots against the marble tiles. A shiver crawled up his spine. Fear curled into a tight fist in his gut. And he knew.

Scott.

Craig walked to the doors, peered through the tiny window, and saw nothing, no one.

Back in the waiting area, he made a pot of coffee. He'd barely raised the cup to his lips when Mike trudged out of ICU looking haggard and concerned. Craig poured another serving of the brew and brought it to Mike.

"How's Scott?"

Mike dry-washed his face and ran a shaky hand through his hair. "I don't know. We're running more tests."

"Was that Code Blue for him?"

Mike swallowed hard, nodded. "Yeah. His heart went into a lethal rhythm. We got him stable again."

"Should I call Trina, or will you?"

Mike shrugged. "Nothing she can do. I say let her rest."

A tired chuckle escaped Craig. "Yeah, and we'll never hear the end of that."

Before he could say more, his cell phone rang. Lexie's name and picture flashed on the screen. "Hey, Lex."

"What's going on? I know something's wrong. Feel it in my gut."

Craig took a deep breath, handed the phone to Mike and listened while he explained Scott's condition and what they were doing to treat him. He bit back a grin when Mike argued with Lexie about her and Trina coming back up in the middle of the night. The grin turned into another tired chuckle when Mike ended the call with a roll of his eyes and a grunt then handed the phone back to him. Craig slid the device into his pocket and asked to see Scott.

"Go on in. I'm going back into the doctor's lounge

to rest awhile before my shift.”

“Not going home?”

Mike shook his head. “Not until he’s out of the woods.”

Craig acknowledged Mike’s declaration with an incline of his head. “Thanks, Mike.”

Mike shrugged. “He’d do the same for me if the situation were reversed.”

“Yes, he would. Get some rest.”

He watched, concerned, as Mike plodded toward the elevators. After he disappeared around the corner, Craig went through the ICU doors and into Scott’s room. He sat beside the bed and put his hand on his friend’s. “Gave everyone a scare there, buddy.”

Scott’s hand twitched.

“I’m here. Trina, Lexie, the boys, and babies are home. You don’t worry about anything, just get yourself better and back to us.”

* * *

Craig awoke groggy and stiff from sleeping in the chair beside Scott's bed, surprised they'd left him there the rest of the night. He watched the monitors a moment. From what he could gather, everything looked OK. He stood, stretched, and walked into the visitor's kitchenette, where he found a fresh pot of coffee brewing—and the pot had a 'sneak a cup' feature. *Thank you, Lord.* He poured a cup then walked to the nurse's station to inquire as to Mike's whereabouts.

"He's still resting in the doctor's lounge."

Craig acknowledged the news with a slight nod, then went back into the visitor's area.

Dawn had hardly broken over the horizon when Lexie entered. Craig enfolded her in a hug.

"How is he?"

"Good. From what I can tell. He passed a peaceful night after the incident."

"That's good to hear. I left Trina and the girls

sleeping. Woke the boys for school but they were surly and uncommunicative. Not sure if they got up and went or not. I wanted to get here and relieve you."

Craig threw his empty Styrofoam container in the trashcan. "I'll get over there now and help Trina deal with the children. She can take a shift later. Call if you need anything, or if there's the slightest change."

He made his way out of the hospital, to the parking garage and into his truck where he sank down into the seat with a sigh. Just for a moment, he indulged in the emotional breakdown he'd fought since Trina's call night before last. A sob rolled through his chest, shuddered there, then broke through his defenses. "God...please..." was all he could manage to pray before the total meltdown.

Spent from the outburst, he started the engine and drove to Scott and Trina's home. He found Trina in a heated battle with Richard over going to school.

"We're already late. Why can't we just stay home

today?"

"Yeah," Robert chimed.

Craig hesitated on approaching until he saw the terror on Trina's ashen face. "Enough, boys."

All eyes turned to him.

"Get your things together and let's go." He walked over and gathered Trina against his chest as the two stomped off, bickering amongst themselves. "I'll take them and talk to the principal."

A violent tremble rattled her. "How is he?"

"He's stable."

She stiffened. "I'm so tired of hearing that phrase. What does it mean, anyway?"

Craig knew he couldn't, shouldn't keep the truth from her. Still, he tried to temper the fear and concern in his voice when he answered. "There was a small incident last night with his heart, but this morning he's resting comfortably."

"How can he be comfortable with all those tubes

and wires? Is he even breathing on his own?"

This he could answer with absolute assurance. "Yes. The ventilator is merely to help so he doesn't have to tax his system. It's taking the strain off his heart and lungs."

The boys appeared, ready—if reluctant—to go to school. Trina disengaged herself from Craig's embrace to hug her sons. "Do your best to have a good day. If anything happens, we'll get you right away."

"Yes ma'am," they mumbled in unison.

She turned back to Craig. "Are you sure you're OK to drive them? I don't want any of you endangered because you've been up there all night."

He ached to his very bones with fatigue and worry. Craig handed her his keys. "You're right. I'll check on the girls then take a shower while you run these two to school. As soon as you return, we'll grab some breakfast, and then I'll get some shut-eye."

He watched until they'd backed out of the drive,

then mounted the stairs and entered Rikki's room where, thankfully, both babies slept soundly. He sank into the rocking chair, rubbed his tired, gritty eyes, and succumbed to the soul-deep weariness.

* * *

Trina pulled into the garage, rested her forehead on the steering wheel and wept. "Oh, God, how am I going to do this?"

Years of praying and trusting, of strength and faith, deserted her. In that moment, she experienced a fear so deep, so raw, she had no idea how to assimilate it. She stumbled from the truck and into the house where peace and quiet soothed the emotions raging in her heart and stilled the thoughts running rampant in her mind. A wail from the nursery spurred her into action. She rushed up the stairs and entered the room as Craig lifted Tamera Joy from the playpen.

Rikki popped up in her toddler bed. "Tamra." She pointed. "Da Da."

Trina lifted her daughter and tucked her on her hip. A smile broke through her tense lips. "No matter how hard we've tried the last couple of years, we can't get her to call Scott 'daddy.' It's been 'Da Da' since she first spoke the words."

Craig laughed and chucked Rikki's chin. "No, sweetheart, Uncle Craig."

She shook her head. Red-gold curls bounced off her shoulders as she reached for him. "Where Da Da?"

In one smooth movement, Craig handed Trina their granddaughter and took Rikki in his arms. He ran her tiny palm over his lips. "Da Da's at work. Rikki hungry?"

She nodded.

Trina switched girls with him again and carried Rikki to the changing table. "Let's get out of this icky pull-up first."

"I'll take this one downstairs to wash and change her. See you two in a bit." He retrieved Tamera's diaper bag and left the room.

"Down. Walk."

Trina chuckled at the insistence in Tamera's voice. She heard the baby's tiny feet hit the floor and Craig cautioning their granddaughter to be careful. She snapped Rikki's pajama bottoms into place and followed, counting along with Craig and Tamera as everyone descended the steps. Once they reached the bottom, he swung Tamera back up onto his hip and carried her into the bathroom.

In the kitchen, Trina settled Rikki into a highchair. Within moments, Craig strapped Tamera into the other chair and turned to her.

"What can I do?"

She set a juice box in front of each girl. "I got this. Get your shower and I'll have breakfast ready when you're done."

"Just toast or something. Can't eat a big meal right before bed."

A half-hour later both girls were fed, cleaned, and dressed. Craig had showered, eaten toast and peanut butter with jam and gone upstairs to rest. Rikki and Tamera played on the floor of the den. Trina curled up on the couch with her Bible and prayer journal and worked out a schedule for her, Craig, and Lexie to take shifts at the hospital.

Scott nor Craig, nor Mike for that matter would want her or Lex out late, so she assigned Craig the night shift. Since Lex was already there, she would relieve her this afternoon but beginning tomorrow, she would drop the boys off and pick them up from school on her way to and from the hospital. That would allow her to be with her children for breakfast and dinner, keeping their routine as close to normal as possible. She called the principal, then Lexie, and arranged for her to pick up the boys this afternoon. At two o'clock, she left the girls in Craig's care and went to the hospital.

"What's the latest, Mike?" she asked when Mike

met her in the waiting room and escorted her in to see Scott.

He scrubbed a hand over his face, his eyes sad, expression concerned. "Right now, he's holding his own."

"Should I be planning a funeral?"

Mike shook his head and visibly fought a shudder. "I honestly don't know."

"What do you mean you don't know? You're his doctor and our friend. I deserve to know the truth!"

Mike touched her arm. "Let's not have this conversation here. I'll meet you in the hallway after your visit is over. Stay optimistic, Trina." He strode from the room.

Trina collapsed onto a chair beside her husband. She took his hand, lifted it to her cheek. "I'm sorry, Scott. I shouldn't be so afraid, but I am. Please, love, give me some sign that you're still with us."

Nothing.

"You hear me. I know you do. Just a little sign. I don't want you to stress or struggle, but I need to know you're coming back to me and the kids."

His hand twitched. Peace enveloped her. Scott's spirit had connected with and spoken to hers. She kissed the back of his hand then his cheek and whispered in his ear. "Thank you, love."

She left the room and met Mike. He led her into the doctor's lounge and prepared her a cup of coffee. "I'm sorry, Mike, for being rude."

His grin came easily. "You weren't rude. I understand how frustrating this can be, but, Trina, I honestly don't know what's next. He's holding his own is *all* I can say. God only knows what was on that knife.

"We're testing him for virus or infection, keeping him on antibiotics to be safe. The heart incident could be just stress or adrenalin or an indication of an underlying problem. We really don't know. Everything in his body—hormones, blood cells, enzymes, are on high alert right now, but that's pretty normal.

"All we can do at this point is wait, watch, pray, and handle any complication if and when it arises. That said, if you feel better or more in control by planning a funeral, then do it."

Trina bit her lip and swallowed the knot of panic in her throat. "No. I'm not giving up on him yet. He'll come back to us. I know he will."

Mike's sigh echoed through the room and spoke volumes. "I hope so. I promise to keep you informed of any change or development outside the norm."

"Can I stay with him longer?"

"Sure, I can let you do that as long as we don't have an emergency situation arise or come in."

"Thank you."

Craig arrived around eight-thirty and insisted she go home. Trina kissed Scott's cheek, promised to see him the next day, and gave in to Craig's urging.

Chapter Four

The days slid by, one into the other. Three...four...five.

Craig, Trina, and Lexie slipped into a routine. The women traded shifts during the day. He stayed every night. The boys came up a time or two. Neither argued to see Scott but both felt better being at the hospital whenever possible. All waited, wondered, and prayed for Scott to wake up. By day eight, everyone was at their wit's end.

Craig rubbed his arm and leaned over Scott. "You know I sat with Ace twenty-four-seven for ten days when he got kicked by that horse...almost five years ago now. I'm not leaving here until you come back to us."

Craig.

He felt more than heard Scott's voice.

"I'm here, buddy."

Scott's eyebrows twitched; mouth moved.

Brother.

Again, the word resonated with Scott's voice, yet no sound escaped his lips.

He and Scott had always been close. Connected at the hip, his grandfather always said. But in that moment, Craig understood they were more connected at the heart. He drug the chair closer to the bed, bowed his head, prayed for guidance, and waited.

Letter.

Craig moved closer, positive he'd heard wrong. "Lexie? You want Lexie to come up?"

He watched Scott for signs that he heard, that he understood. A deep breath shuddered through Scott and the monitors connected to him went ballistic. Hospital staff rushed in and drove Craig out.

"What happened?"

Craig turned at the sound of his daughter-in-law's voice. "I,—" He shook his head and raked his fingers through his hair. "I don't know. We were...talking..."

"He spoke? He's awake?"

"No." No words had left Scott's mouth, but he knew, somehow, someway, his friend had spoken to him. "It's weird, or maybe I'm just tired and imagining things, but I swear I heard him say my name and a couple of other words."

A frown marred Lexie's forehead. "That makes no sense. What's going on now?"

"I don't know. He took one deep breath, then the monitors went crazy. They ran me out. What are you doing here this time of night?"

"I couldn't sleep."

"Lexie…"

She held up a hand, halting his words. "I know what you're going to say but I'm here so save your breath." She stifled a sob. "I can't bear this."

"You need to go home."

"He's the only real father I've known. I can't leave him. Why don't you go on to the house and get some rest?"

Mike had finally given in and gone home earlier so the on-call doctor came into the waiting room and informed them Scott was resting and stable once more. Craig sat with Lexie for a while then caved to her insistence and went back to Scott's house.

** * **

Ace flew in for the weekend and Lexie picked him up at the airport. After a quick trip to the hospital to see Trina and check on Scott, they went to the house so Ace could spend some time with his father and daughter. Robert flew into his embrace.

"Uncle Ace!"

Ace hugged him. "Hey, buddy. How's it going?"

His lip trembled. Tears filled his eyes. "Not sure. We don't know how daddy's doing."

Ace gave him a squeeze. "He's still holding his own right now. All we can do is pray. You're praying, aren't you?"

Robert nodded.

"Where's Ritchie?"

"Don't call me Ritchie."

The tone of his voice ripped through Ace's heart. Gone was the boy he'd known, loved, and teased since birth. In his place stood an arrogant adolescent. Ace offered his hand instead of a hug. "Sorry 'bout that. How are you, Richard?"

Richard shrugged and stomped away.

Ace glanced at Lexie, saw the fear and concern in her gaze.

"He's so angry."

He lifted a brow. "More than that, I bet."

Lexie nodded. "Yeah, he's afraid. We all are, but every time we try to comfort or reassure him, he gets all bent out of shape. Your dad's the only one who has even a smidgen of control over him."

"I'll try to talk with him later. Where's....?" Before

he could finish asking, Craig walked into the room and hugged Ace tight against his chest. The weariness in his father's face concerned Ace more than Richard's belligerence. An hour later, after he convinced the older man to get some rest, Ace found Richard up in his room. Brooding.

"What's with the 'tude, dude?"

Richard rolled his eyes and snorted. "I'm tired of everyone treating me like a baby."

"From what I hear you're acting like one. A spoiled, bratty one at that."

Richard's defiance fled in the face of Ace's disappointment. His chin dropped, eyes lowered, lips trembled. "What if he dies?"

Ace arched a brow at him. "What if he doesn't? You think he'll be proud of the way you've manned up and helped your mother?"

Richard swallowed, hard. Shame brightened the dark eyes. Much as he wanted to, Ace refrained from coddling the boy. "I know you're scared, buddy. We all are. But you'd better get a grip. Whether Scott lives or dies, you'll be the one living with the consequences of your actions. You want to be dependable in a crisis. An asset, not a liability. Capiche?"

Richard nodded.

Years of affection won out over discipline. Ace pulled him into a hug. "Good. Now let's go see about rustling up some food. I'm starving."

* * *

Not much changed over the next couple of days. Scott's heart wavered as though he struggled with the desire to stay. Or leave. The family took turns sitting with him. Ace took a shift also, giving everyone else a break. He carried the chair closer to the bed, rested his head on fists, and prayed.

Ace.

His head jerked up. "I'm here, Scott."

Moments passed with no indication Scott had

actually spoken. Shaking off the eerie feeling that he was losing his mind, Ace returned to the prayerful pose.

Lex.

Ace startled to attention again. "Lexie's fine, Scott. She and the boys, Tamera Joy, Trina, and Rikki Jayne, everyone's fine. Even daddy. It's you we're worried about. We need you back, buddy."

Again, nothing—no indication Scott had roused enough to speak. A flash of understanding quickened Ace's spirit. Since his time in a coma, Ace knew better than most the spiritual realm was closer than many understood—a thought, a whisper away.

"OK, Scott. I get it. You're trying to communicate with me the best way you can. I'm here, buddy. I'm listening."

Ace folded his hands once more and bowed his head. He took several deep breaths, allowed his heart, mind, and spirit to open, focused solely on Scott, then waited.

Craig. Trina. Letter. Promise.

Elation swept through him as the words echoed loud and clear in his soul, followed by a wave of sadness when Scott's heart monitor went haywire. Doctors and nurses rushed in and shoved him out of the room.

"Call Trina," Mike barked. "Get her here now!"

Ace stumbled into the hallway, clawed his cell phone from his pocket, and called his father. Whether moments or an eternity later, he didn't know, but the entire family filed into the waiting area. A flurry of questions ensued, bombarding him from every direction.

"What happened?" Trina asked, followed by Craig's "What's going on?" and Lexie's, "How is he?"

All Ace could do was shake his head and shrug. *Although he knew....*

Mike exited Scott's room. Tears streamed from his eyes. Sobs shook his frame. "I... We... He's..."

With a keening wail, Trina crumbled into a chair.

Chaos ensued.

Babies cried. Lexie clung to the boys. Craig embraced his son.

Mike sat beside Trina and put an arm around her shoulder. "You want to see him?"

She nodded.

"Me too," the boys cried in unison.

Mike stood, hesitated. "Give me a minute to check on him and I'll come get y'all." He wanted to make sure the nurses had removed the wires and tubes and transferred Scott into a private isolation room, where his family would be able to visit with him for as long as they needed to say goodbye. Within moments, he ushered Trina in.

In his years as a physician, Mike had often witnessed misery and miracles, but neither had affected him on a personal level. He stood, shattered, and watched Trina sob into Scott's shoulder, pound on his chest, and beg him not to leave her and the kids.

Scott's body twitched. Breath shuddered through him. His arm wound around Trina and, just like that, he was back.

Mike rushed over and took his pulse. Weak. Sporadic. "Scott," he whispered, afraid to hope. "Can you hear me, buddy?"

Nothing.

Trina lifted a stricken gaze to his. The devastation in her eyes ripped his heart. "What just happened?"

Mike shrugged. "I don't know, but we've got a pulse. Let's bring the kids in just in case this is temporary."

Trina nodded.

Mike went into the lobby and gathered Scott's family. He explained what happened but cautioned them against getting their hopes up. One by one they entered the room and circled the bed. Richard and Robert, Lexie and Ace—each holding a baby—and finally, Craig.

Richard leaned close to Scott's ear. "Daddy?"

Nothing.

Robert did the same, touching Scott's hand. "We're here, Daddy. Please wake up."

Rikki struggled against Lexie's grasp. "Da Da."

Lexie brought her sister closer and encouraged her to kiss Scott.

Rikki placed both hands on Scott's cheeks and pressed tiny kisses to his face murmuring, "Da Da," all the while, yet Scott never flinched. His chest rose and fell with an occasional breath.

A nurse entered the room and informed Mike of an approaching ambulance. Before he went to tend to the patient coming in, he left strict orders that Scott's family not be disturbed and asked for more chairs to be brought in. Two hours later, he returned to find no change in Scott's condition. His pulse beat in an erratic thud and breath came in shallow gasps with long stretches of silence in-between. He wasn't dead, yet Mike couldn't quite say Scott lived.

For hours they stayed, Lexie or Trina leaving the room only when necessary to tend to a child. After nearly six hours of waiting, Craig pulled Mike aside.

"What's going on?"

Mike rubbed his tired, gritty eyes and shrugged. "All I can say is he's holding on. He's totally in God's hands now. The entire family can stay as long as they like, but these little ones will get restless."

"True, but I doubt you'd be able to run anyone out even with the threat of violent force."

A weary chuckle escaped Mike. "Well, I'll continue to be in and out as much as I can while working the ER, but if anything changes, have me paged right away."

"Will do."

As the evening wore on, the babies wore out. Scott's daughter and granddaughter were laid on the bed beside him, each tiny, red-gold head resting against his chest. Craig and Ace took turns hustling the boys out to stretch their legs, get snacks, or whatever.

Eight hours passed...ten...twelve, and still, no change. Then, as dawn broke over the horizon and slivers of light peeked through the blinds and painted the room in a soft, warm glow, Scott crossed into the spiritual realm.

Craig put his arms around Richard and Robert while Ace and Lexie gathered up the babies and the lot of them left the room.

Mike allowed Trina a few more minutes, then drew her gently to her feet and escorted her out. He stopped at the nurse's station and whispered for them to call the coroner.

* * *

After everyone loaded into the Suburban, Craig took the keys. Amongst muffled sobs from the boys, Lex and Trina, the atmosphere was thick with despair. Trina cuddled her sons and, once home, walked with them to their room. Ace and Lexie tended to the babies, but Craig was alone. He went into the den, found a decanter of Bourbon, and poured a liberal amount into a jigger. Sinking onto the couch, he drank. Warmth spread through his body as the liquid slid down his throat, but nothing could ease the chill in his soul. Finally, the tears came…huge, heaving sobs that vibrated his very bones. "Oh…God…."

"Craig."

He froze. Took another drink, certain he'd lost, or would soon lose, his mind. That was Scott's voice. His presence filled the room.

"What is it, buddy?"

"Trina…letter…promise."

"You don't have to worry about Trina and the kids, buddy. I remember my promise." Craig finished his drink, poured another, and waited. No other communication ensued.

He took the glass to the kitchen, placed it in the sink, and climbed the stairs to the guest room he'd occupied for the last two weeks.

Chapter Five

The next morning everyone dragged themselves downstairs, the boys sullen and uncommunicative. Trina wept quiet tears, uttering soft sobs, while she set about preparing breakfast. Lexie made phone calls and scheduled an appointment with the funeral home for later that afternoon.

After everyone had eaten, they sat around the table discussing arrangements. Scott had asked to be cremated but Trina decided they'd have a full funeral before that, giving everyone a chance to say goodbye. Scott had been deeply loved and respected in the community and at the hospitals where he'd lived and worked for the past two decades. She took notes of what each child wanted for their father, adding suggestions from Craig and Ace. Stanley and Amber would arrive late afternoon/early evening. He'd graciously agreed to sing at Scott's service.

When the house was quiet, the women gone to the funeral home, boys in their room and girls down for a nap, Craig and Ace sat together in the den.

"How're you holding up, Daddy?"

Craig shrugged. "I don't know. Sometimes I feel as if I'm losing it. I keep hearing his voice but what he says makes no sense to me at all."

"What is he saying?"

"Trina and promise...I get that. I assured him years ago if anything happened to him, I'd take care of them. I wouldn't, couldn't, do less. But what is confusing as hell is the word, 'letter'."

"Funny, he said the same thing to me." Ace nodded when Craig's surprised gaze met his. "Right before..."

Craig hugged his son. "I'm sorry you were the one with him when this happened, son. Wish I knew what the hell..." His eyes widened as Scott's meaning suddenly became clear. "His mother's letter. It has to be."

"What letter?"

"Scott's mother left a letter for him to open upon her death. For years he put it off. But sometime after 9-11, he decided it was time. He told me at Christmas that same year that when he died, it was to come to me."

The doorbell pealed, interrupting their conversation. Craig answered and led Mike into the den. "You look like you need a drink."

"I wouldn't turn one down."

Craig poured until liquor danced at the rim of three small goblets. He passed one to Mike, then Ace. They toasted Scott and downed the drink. He poured another.

"Better not have too many of these or I'll never make it home," Mike mumbled before lifting the beaker to his lips.

"You haven't been home yet?"

"No, worked an all-nighter again. The hospital has been searching for someone to fill in for Scott since the incident. We've had to work longer shifts until the new doctor starts next week."

"Any idea who did this, Mike? The patient's name or how he's doing. What'll happen to him now?" Craig asked.

"I can't say. HIPPA laws, ya know."

"And you know nothing you say will go past this room." Ace interjected before Craig could protest.

"I know that, but I'm still bound by law, ethics, morality..." Mike hesitated, sipped again. "But I will say this: Trina needs to be very aware of her circumstances and who's around her at all times, from here on out."

"You think she's in danger? From whom?"

Mike's gaze met Craig's in a long, drawn-out pause. "Who do you know that would harm her? Especially now that Scott isn't around."

It took less than a heartbeat for them to get what Mike hinted at.

Craig downed the rest of his drink. "I'll kill him

first."

Ace vaulted from his chair and paced the room. "How can we protect her? Them? We live a day's drive from here."

"We'll figure it out," Craig assured. "Trina has to know. After all this is over, I'll tell her and together, we'll figure something out. Is Jack Simmons still in the hospital?"

"Yeah. He'll be there for at least thirty days, possibly longer, if he lives through detox. It can be hell and he's not doing too well. Scott's death has been reported and Jack charged with murder, so once he's out of the hospital he'll probably go straight to jail."

"Will you keep me posted?"

"I'll do my best, but I'd suggest Trina visit a lawyer and perhaps the police department. File a restraining order."

"Hire a bodyguard, more like it," Ace muttered. His one encounter with Trina's ex-husband nearly a dozen years ago had left an indelible mark on his young mind.

A wail from the nursery followed by lusty cries jolted Ace into action. He took the stairs two at a time and gathered his daughter into his arms.

Rikki sat up in her bed, rubbed her eyes, and held out her hands. "Up."

"Hang tight, sweetheart. Uncle Ace has to tend to Tamera first."

Her tiny lip quivered. "I want up. Out."

Ace called for Richard who answered with a grunted, "What?"

"Come in here and pick your sister up, that's what! Now, please."

Richard slammed out of his room and stomped toward the bed. By the look on his face, he was all set to jerk Rikki up.

"Bu-ba," she cooed.

He melted. "Hey, sweet girl, what'cha want?"

"I want up."

"Gently," Ace advised, pleased when Richard cuddled the little one tenderly against his chest. His heart shattered when the teenage boy buried his face in his sister's hair and crumbled. Ace finished changing Tamera's clothes, wet from a leaky pull-up, then closed the distance between him and Richard and embraced the pair.

"He—he's—really—g—gone."

"Yeah, buddy. He is. But we're here for you. For all of you," he added as Robert joined them, sobs shaking his entire frame.

Rikki squirmed in Richard's arms and patted his cheeks. "Don't cwy, Bu-ba." She did the same to Robert. "It OK, Bobert."

Her sweet voice and innocent gestures eased the tumultuous emotions. Both boys swiped a sleeve across their eyes and nose.

Richard gazed up at Ace. "How are we—how's *Mama* ever going to get through this?"

Ace gave him a squeeze. "It won't be easy, that's for sure. All any of us can do, is keep living. One day at a time.

Rikki bounced on her brother's hip. "I needa go potty."

"Like a big girl?" Richard asked.

She nodded.

He let her slide from his arms and took her by the hand. "OK, let's go."

Ace shifted his daughter. "We should try to potty too. We'll meet you guys downstairs. Dr. Guidry is here. I'm sure he'd love to see y'all."

The boys murmured their agreement, and everyone exited the room.

* * *

The next few days passed in a blur of tears and activity. People came and went, bringing food, comfort, and condolences. The new physician arrived early, giving Mike much-needed time off. He spent the majority of it helping the family field calls and accept deliveries—basically doing what he could to aide his best friend's family.

The ceremony was as lovely an affair as wakes could be. The small funeral home where Scott lay in repose stayed packed, wall-to-wall at all times with acquaintances, co-workers, and colleagues. Before they were ready, the time came to say their final farewells.

And then it was all over.

Two days later Craig and Trina sat at the kitchen table in a too-quiet house. Amber, Stanley, and their children had left early Sunday morning to return to Bandera. After much discussion and coaxing, Ace, Lexie, and Tamera left this morning after the boys reluctantly caught the bus for school. They'd yet to determine when or how Craig would go home.

A wail from the den pierced the silence. Before Katrina could get out of her chair, Rikki raced into the room and into her mother's arms.

"What's the matter, baby?"

"I wanna pway wit Tamra."

"Tamra went home to Texas with her mommy and daddy."

"Wit Wexie and Ace?"

"Yeah. Would you like to watch a movie?"

She rubbed her eyes and sniffled. "I want Da Da."

Trina stroked her daughter's silky, red-gold hair. "I know, baby. I do too, but Da Da's in heaven. He's an angel now and he's watching over us. How 'bout we watch Veggie Tales?"

Rikki brightened. A smile replaced the quivering lips. "Yeah, Beggie Tales."

Katrina carried her daughter back into the den and set the movie on to play then brought Rikki a cup of warm milk. Once the child rested comfortably against a huge bean bag chair, covered with her blankey and cuddling a stuffed rabbit, Trina returned to the table.

Silence ensued once more, then she gazed up at Craig.

"What now?"

Craig placed his hand over hers, stilling Trina's nervous shredding of a napkin. "You have a lot of legal details to tend to. You'll need to make an appointment with your lawyer to have Scott's will read, call the Social Security office and file for benefits for yourself and the children. I'm sure he's also got investments and life insurance policies or annuities meant to support y'all."

"I don't know if I can do this, Craig." Her voice broke on a sob.

"There's nothing easy about it, but your children need you now more than ever. When Tamera died, mine were grown. Well, practically. As you know, Ace was a senior in high-school and Amber already married with two children. They weren't as dependent on me as yours are on you. I can stay as long as you want and help you through all of this."

"It's hard to believe she's been gone eight years."

"Feels like yesterday, especially now."

Trina acknowledged his comment with a tiny nod. A knock on the door halted their words. Craig opened it to Mike, who walked in and hugged Trina.

"How're you holding up?"

Trina shrugged and shook her head but before she could answer, the phone rang. She rushed into the kitchen to answer. "Oh, my. Yes, yes, I'll be right there."

Craig and Mike waited for her to return. What had happened now? She walked out of the kitchen rubbing at the frown on her forehead.

"What is it?" Craig asked.

"Robert had a meltdown. Richard got in a fight. Will....?"

"I'll watch Rikki," Craig answered before she could finish the question.

"Thanks. I'll be right back. Make yourself at home, Mike. There's fresh coffee unless you have to get to work soon."

"Thanks. I'll stay a while and visit with Craig. Be careful. We'll see you and the boys when you get back."

The two men watched her hurry through the garage door. "I'll check on Rikki while you get your coffee," Craig said.

"Sure. Want me to refresh yours?"

"That'd be great. Thanks."

"She's out like a light," Craig said with a chuckle when they were seated once more.

"The joy of innocence," Mike remarked. "She's such a beautiful child, so much like her mother."

Craig arched a brow but refrained from comment.

"You tell her about Jack yet?"

Craig squirmed. "I was hoping to avoid that for a few days at least. How is he?"

"About the same. In and out of consciousness. Combative when in, barely hanging on when out."

"Maybe we'll get lucky and she won't have to know at all."

"Perhaps, but better to be safe than sorry and tell her before she finds out some other way."

Craig's sigh spoke volumes. "I know. Hopefully, I can at least put it off until they come to Bandera for Easter and Spring break."

"You think she'll still go?"

"I hope so."

"It'd probably be better than Lexie trying to come here in her condition. How far along is she now?"

"Four and a half, five months."

The small talk continued until Trina returned with the boys, everyone tense and sulking.

"You two go on up to your rooms. We'll talk about this later," Trina said.

"Yes ma'am," they muttered in unison and then trudged up the stairs.

Trina slid into a chair.

"Looks like you could use a drink," Mike said, a hint of teasing in his tone.

She smiled. "I could, but coffee will have to do for now."

"I'll get it," Craig offered and stood to do so. He brought the mug back and set it in front of her.

"I guess I should keep the boys home this week or at least a couple more days."

"Probably wouldn't hurt." Mike rose from his seat. "I need to get on home. How long you gonna be here?" he asked Craig.

"As long as she needs me to be."

"OK. Guess I'll see you around then." He bent and pressed his lips to Trina's forehead. "You take care and if there's anything I can do, let me know."

Trina thanked him and he let himself out.

Chapter Six

For the next several days Trina worked to settle herself and the children into some sort of routine as they adjusted to their new normal. She kept the boys home from school the rest of that week but picked up and dropped off their homework daily. She ran errands and attended appointments, ironing out and wrapping up details from Scott's estate. At night she'd settle into their king-sized bed and cry herself to sleep, only to get up the next morning and go through the motions all over again.

The following Monday she insisted Richard and Robert return to school and cautioned them with dire consequences should she be called in for anything but an emergency. Then she picked up Scott's ashes from the funeral parlor, took them home, and indulged in the first total meltdown since his death.

Craig pushed a shot of Amaretto, the only liquor

she truly enjoyed, into her hand.

"It's too early," she protested.

"Never too early. Trust me, I know."

She took a tentative taste. "I'm afraid I won't stop at just one."

"That's OK too. I'm here and I'll take care of Rikki and pick up the boys from school if you need me to. You've earned the right to get tore up from the floor up as the young people say." He chuckled, glad when a giggle escaped her trembling lips.

"In that case...." She downed the contents and held the glass out for a refill.

Craig obliged.

"I think I'll just take this up to my room." Trina clasped the pewter urn to her breast, took the bottle from him with one hand, her drink in the other, and turned away.

Craig watched her ascend the stairs, his heart breaking for the woman he'd come to love as much as he had his brother. Not wanting to add to her burden, he hadn't asked her yet about Scott's mother's letter. She'd get to it sooner or later without him bothering her about it. For the next several hours he ran back and forth up the stairs, checking on Trina and taking care of Rikki. At two-thirty he loaded the baby up in her car seat and went to pick up the boys.

"Where's Mama?" Robert wanted to know.

"She's at home, not feeling too well today."

Although Rikki kept up a steady stream of chatter, the boys remained silent except for a few grunts and smiles in answer to her questions. They'd barely made it into the kitchen and settled for a snack when a wail and the sound of breaking crystal shattered the atmosphere.

Craig raced up the stairs two at a time and enfolded Trina against his chest where she soaked his shirt with tears.

Richard and Robert appeared at the doorway, pale and shaken.

"Is she all right?" Robert asked.

Craig swallowed the lump in his throat and tried to alleviate their fears. "She's having a bad day. She'll be okay though. One of you needs to go down and stay with your sister."

"You go." Richard gave his brother a nudge with his elbow as Trina wretched into the garbage can by the bed. "What's going on?"

"Get her a wet washcloth and some water." Craig kept a tight grip on her so that Trina didn't fall out of the bed.

Richard brought the items, gagging at the putrid odor filling the room. "She's drunk?"

Trina rinsed her mouth, wiped a hand over it, and then buried her face in the cool cloth. "Yes, she's drunk and pissed. I want to know why this has happened to me. To us. Who did this and why Scott had to be the one to get hurt and die!"

"We'll talk about that later, Trina," Craig said, his

tone gentle.

She glared up at him. "What do you mean? You know something I don't?" She tossed the cloth down and grabbed his arm. "What do you know? I deserve the truth."

"And you'll get it, but not right here, right now."

She shoved away from Craig and stumbled to her feet. "Oh yes, right here and right now. How dare you keep anything from me?"

Craig stood to face her wrath. "I'd hoped to spare you."

"Spare me from what?"

He softened his words to temper the blow. "It's Jack."

She paled and swayed. "My Jack? My ex-husband Jack?"

Richard took a step closer. "What do you mean your ex-husband? You were married before? How come we didn't know that?"

Trina reached for her son, gasping when he recoiled from her touch. "I didn't think you needed to know, that's why."

He flung around, then turned on her in an angry whirl. "All your talk about purity and honesty and you've been married before? You're nothing but a lying, cheating, fornicating hypocrite!"

Trina's eyes widened; surprised shock lined her face. "Do you even know what that word means?"

Richard sneered. "Yeah, I know what it means. It means f...."

Craig jerked him up by the collar. "Don't you even let that word slip through your mouth," he warned, his teeth clenched as tightly as the fist wrapped in the material on Richard's neck. "One more word out of you and you'll not only be spittin' suds, you won't be able to sit for a month."

"Enough," Trina shouted when Richard turned a pale shade of green and shivered. She stepped between them as Craig released the boy. "Go to your room, Richard. Now. We'll talk later." She turned to Craig. "And you..."

"Trina, I'm..."

She held up a hand to ward off any further comments. "I think it's time you go home."

"I'm not leaving you alone with those children unless, *until* I know you're safe."

"Where is Jack now?"

"He's still in detox."

Trina sank onto the bed. "What'll happen once he's out?"

"He'll probably go straight to jail. But there's no telling for how long."

"Mike told you this and he didn't tell me?"

"We didn't want to add the weight of that burden to everything else you've been going through. I intended to tell you but hoped to put it off until y'all came to Bandera in a couple of weeks."

"Oh, God... Oh, my God," she moaned, clutching her stomach.

Craig reached for her, but she brushed him off. He picked up the rag, cup, and trashcan and carried them into the bathroom. He rinsed the washcloth and cup, refilled it and carried both to Trina. He returned to the bathroom, cleaned the trashcan, and then set it down by the bed.

He sat next to her. "I'll go with you to the police department tomorrow and we'll see what all needs to be done. Once I feel sure you and the kids are safe, I'll go home if you still want me to."

"I don't know what I want right now." She curled into a fetal position on the bed.

"Fair enough. I'll tend to the children tonight and we can talk about it tomorrow." His heart heavy, Craig left her alone. He closed the door behind him and went downstairs.

* * *

Trina fought a sense of unease when Richard didn't come down for breakfast and refused to panic even after finding his room empty and backpack gone. He sometimes got up early and caught a ride to school with friends—although he usually left a note. Trina brushed that off, figuring he was still upset about last night. Unease turned to fear in the span of a breath when the call from school came, informing her he hadn't shown up.

"Richard's not at school."

"What?" Craig had barely made it through the door after dropping Robert off. He turned around. "I'll find him."

"No, let me." Trina held out her hand. "I know all of his favorite places to hang out."

Craig handed her the keys. "Be careful."

She returned thirty minutes later in a full-blown panic. "I can't find him anywhere! Oh, God, what's happened to my son? This is all your fault. You should have never put your hands on him last night."

"The boy needs discipline."

"The boy needs compassion. He just lost his father!"

"You've lost your husband, and I, my brother. That's no excuse to disrespect you the way he's done since this whole ordeal began. Now, give me the keys. I'll go look some more." Craig caught the ring of metal in mid-air when she tossed them toward him. "Let me know if he calls."

He slammed out the door and made the hospital his first stop. Mike met him in the lobby when Craig had him paged. "I'm just about to leave. What's up?"

Craig explained the situation. Mike called the other hospitals in Lafayette as well as the police department, but no one had a record of Richard being there, nor a teenage John Doe.

Chapter Seven

Richard huddled onto a bench, cold, frightened, and hungry. People walked past. Some ignored him. Others eyed him in a way that made him want to squirm. Or melt into the concrete on which he sat. Now that he'd cooled off, he realized just how much danger, not to mention trouble, he was in. He took his cell phone from his jacket pocket, relieved to find it had a signal and enough of a charge to make at least one call.

Lexie answered with a smile in her voice. "Hey, Richard, how's it going?"

"Can you buy me a ticket to come see you?"

"What? Where are you?"

"At the bus station."

"What on earth are you doing there?"

"We got home yesterday to find Mama drunk on her ass and puking her guts out. Did you know she was married before?"

* * *

Lexie snapped her fingers at Ace who was headed out the back door and waved him over. She put the phone down and on speaker. "No, I didn't know she was married before. What's that got to do with you being at the bus station?"

"Craig threatened to beat me within inches of my life. I won't go back. Will you buy me a ticket or not? I need to figure out what I'm going to do."

Lexie took a deep breath and picked up the phone. "Let me get online and check tickets. Don't go anywhere, do you hear me?"

"Yeah."

"Promise, Richard."

"I promise."

"OK, I'll call you back in a bit." She put the phone down and laid her head beside it.

Ace rubbed her back. "Deep breaths, Lex. I'm calling Daddy." He dug out his cell and punched in numbers.

"Did you hear what he said about your father threatening him?"

"I doubt Daddy would do that unless provoked pretty badly. He never disciplined us with more than a few harsh words or a swat on the behind when we were little. Hey, Dad..."

* * *

Mike waited for Craig to hang up the phone. He did so with a heavy exhale.

"That was Ace. Richard called Lexie. He's at the bus station."

"Let me get him. He may not take too well to seeing you right now and he's liable to be upset with his sister for calling you. I'll bring him home in a bit."

Craig agreed and left for Trina's house.

Mike ran back into the hospital, collected his things, and headed to the bus station, praying Richard would still be there. He found the boy sitting on a bench in a far corner of the covered patio. Buses lined the pick-up/drop off area. He sat beside Richard. "Hey, buddy. Heard you had some trouble last night."

"Lexie called you?"

"No. Craig told me. He's been all over town looking for you. Want to fill me in on what the problem is?"

"Just found out my mother is a drunk and a liar."

Mike bit back his fury at the boy's declaration. "Doesn't sound like the woman I know. Care to elaborate?"

"Did *you* know she was married before?"

"That's what this is all about?"

"Among other things. She never told us."

Mike removed a folder he'd stashed in his jacket, opened it, and laid it on the concrete between them. Richard glanced down, turned a shade whiter than Mike's lab coat, and swallowed hard.

"Is that Mama?"

"No, that's your grandmother."

"What happened?"

"Trina's stepfather fell off the wagon. He committed suicide a few days after Elizabeth's funeral." Mike took out another folder and opened it up.

Richard made a strangled sound, and then huge, heaving sobs rattled his entire frame.

"Do you understand now why she may not have felt the need to tell her children about a previous marriage to someone who could hurt her again?" Mike paused. "Or maybe hurt them?"

The kid nodded.

"Think you can give her a break now?"

Richard's phone rang. Too choked up to speak, he handed it to Mike.

"Yeah, I'm with him now. He's fine. No, I don't think he'll need that ticket. Will you, Richard?"

Richard shook his head.

"I'm sure he'll call you later. Yes, I'll tell him. Take care of yourself. See you soon." Mike hung up and handed the phone back to the boy.

"Ready to go home or do you want a bite of breakfast first?"

"Wish you could just drop me off at school, so I don't have to face them yet."

"I can do that. Let's go."

Mike waited with Richard while the principal called Katrina and then allowed Mike to sign him in. Afterward, he went back to the hospital, returned the charts to Medical Records, and then headed to Scott's house. He spent the day with Trina and Craig, discussing Trina's options, and waited with Craig when she went to pick the boys up from school.

An air of tension surrounded the family as they entered through the kitchen door. "Robert, please get your snack and go on to your room. The rest of us have a few things to discuss. I know, life's not fair," Trina remarked in response to his grumbling.

She addressed her oldest son as he started toward

the stairs. "Would you like a snack, Richard?"

Richard turned to face them. His jaw muscle twitched as he visibly strove to control his emotions. "No, ma'am."

Before Katrina could say another word, he broke. "I'm sorry, Mama…" He brushed at the tears streaming down his cheeks. "I apologize to you too, Uncle Craig."

His drenched eyes beseeched each of them in turn. "Dr. Guidry, thank you for coming to get me and for setting me straight. I'll try to be more compassionate before jumping to conclusions or judging others."

Craig rose and embraced the boy. "That's all any of us can ask or do."

Trina hugged him also. "Supper will be ready in a couple of hours. You sure you don't want a snack?"

"I'm sure. I'll see if Robert needs any help with his homework."

"Thank you."

A collective sigh heaved throughout the room when Richard clomped up the stairs and into his brother's room. Trina invited Mike to stay for supper and accepted both men's help in preparing the food and setting the table. Though a bit subdued, the meal proved a pleasant affair.

Chapter Eight

Craig settled into his favorite chair. *It is so good to be home.* He smiled at his son when he walked into the room and sighed in appreciation when Ace handed him a jigger of Brandy.

"To home," he said and clinked glasses with Ace.

"How're you doing, Daddy?"

Craig moved his chair into a reclining position, rested his head against the back of it, and shrugged. "I doubt everything has really had a chance to sink in yet with all of the craziness these past few weeks."

"I hear ya. Kinda figured that's the way it would be. I'm here for you though. We all are."

"I know that son, but it's nice to hear."

"How's Trina holding up? Really?"

"Better these last couple of weeks."

"And Jack?"

"Last word, he's still in the detox unit. Mike is

keeping us updated as much as he can. Trina's been in touch with the law and her attorney."

"Guess the best we can hope for is he goes to jail for a long time."

Craig grunted. "The best we can hope for is the bastard leaves the hospital in a body bag."

"Yeah, I thought that too, but Lexie and Trina both believe as long as he's alive there's hope God can reach him."

Craig snapped the foot of the recliner into place and lunged from the chair. "Good for them. I don't feel so generous right now."

Ace held out his glass for a refill. "Me either. Guess we're not as loving and compassionate as they are if we're thinking eye for an eye instead of forgiveness."

"Forgiveness is all fine, good and well, son. I'm sure I'll get there at some point, but right now I'd like to tear him apart, limb by limb, with my bare hands."

Ace raised his tumbler in salute. "Ditto."

They turned when Lexie walked in carrying Tamera Joy, all bathed and powdered and ready for bed. "Someone's ready for her bedtime story."

Craig downed the remainder of his drink and held out his arms to his granddaughter. "C'mon, sweetheart, PaPaw will read to you."

She cuddled him a moment then blew kisses to her parents. "Night, night Mommy. Night, night, Daddy."

After kisses and hugs were shared, Craig carried the baby upstairs. He picked up the book off the bedside table, settled into the rocking chair and read until the child drifted off to dream in his arms. Shifting her in his embrace, he stroked her back when she fussed and then settled her into bed but stood a long while gazing at the little beauty who bore his wife's name. Grief struck his heart, so strong, so profound it nearly drove him to his knees. He sank back into the chair and let the tears fall.

* * *

Laughter rang out in the bright, sunny day as

children of all ages set about hunting eggs and searching for prizes. Lexie and Trina helped Tamera and Rikki while Amber assisted her and Stanley's son, William, who was almost five, gather as many of the decorative eggs as they could. At nine, their twins, Ashlyn and Kaitlyn, as well as Robert looked for plastic globes filled with more age-appropriate gifts which were hidden around the yard and in the barn.

Richard hung around the porch feeling at once too old to play the games, and yet too young to be sitting with the men. Ace embraced him in something between a bear hug and a headlock.

"Hey, buddy, you're welcome to hang out here with us old folks, but I have it on good authority some of those golden eggs have cold, hard cash stashed in them."

"Unless it's hundred-dollar bills, I'm not interested."

Ace chuckled. "You never know. Your choice. How's

school going?"

Richard winced. "Be glad when it's over."

"Got a few years before that."

He frowned. "I mean for the summer. Then we can come back here and get Mama away from that maniac she was married to."

"Let's not go there today." The plea in Craig's voice could not be misunderstood.

"Sorry." He lifted wide eyes to Ace. "I just want to protect her, you know."

"Hey, no worries," Ace said. "We're right there with you, bud. But let's try to forget all the bad stuff, at least for a little while today. Now..." He whispered something in Richard's ear.

Richard arched a brow in interest. "Really? Care to give me a hint where?"

Ace laughed. "Nope, you're on your own."

He rolled his eyes and headed for the barn.

Stanley kicked back in his chair. "Poor kid, stuck

between being a child and manhood."

Craig tilted his chair back, resting it against the window ledge. "Yep, got a rude awakening to some of the harsh realities of life these last few weeks."

"Adversity builds character. He'll be fine. We've all got some baggage from our childhood or teenage years and we've turned out pretty well." Stan winked at his brother-in-law. "Most of us anyway," he added with a grin.

Craig grunted. "Knew I'd rue the day I didn't run you off with a shotgun."

One by one the youngsters grew tired of traipsing the property in search of Easter treasures. Mother's soothed fussy babies. Father's 'oohed' and 'aahed' over the older kids' haul.

Craig laughed at the antics, but the ache in his heart remained a stark reminder that two of his pack were missing.

* * *

The next few days passed in a flurry of activity. As the time for Trina and the kids to return home drew nearer, Richard became more and more adamant they stay in Bandera. So much so that Trina had extended their vacation to encompass the boys' entire Spring Break. They'd finished breakfast and were packing to leave the B&B when he voiced his opinion against returning home once more.

"You've only got a few weeks of school left," she argued.

"I know that—and then we're going to turn around and come right back here. Can't you get our lessons from school and we can do them from home?"

"I don't think that's possible. Besides, don't y'all have your annual LEAP tests soon?"

"Who cares about that junk? Wish we could just move here."

Trina arched a brow at him. "Seriously?"

"Yeah. Do you think it's possible?"

Trina plopped into a chair at the table and waited for him to sit before continuing. "It's always possible but I doubt it would happen so quickly that you couldn't finish school. What's really bothering you, baby?"

Frustration lit his gaze, but Richard wisely took a breath and bit back his normal retort at her use of the word 'baby.' "Mama, I know your ex-husband was abusive to you and I think you...we all would be safer here."

"Who told you that?"

"Dr. Guidry told me."

"Well, he shouldn't have, and I'll be sure to inform him of that myself."

A knock on the door interrupted their discussion.

"Come in," Trina called.

Craig and Lexie waked through.

"Came to see if y'all needed some help getting things together and loading up," Craig offered, then frowned. "Something wrong?"

"I just found out Mike told my fourteen-year-old son intimate details about my previous marriage. Things that should fall under patient/doctor confidentiality."

Craig stroked a hand down her hair in a soothing gesture. "I'm sure Mike meant no harm in telling him. Technically Richard is the man of the house now."

The glare she bestowed on him should have singed Craig's flesh. "*Technically*, Richard is still *my* child. It is not his place to protect me, but mine to protect him and his brother and sister. Which I am one-hundred-percent capable of doing."

A quick look from Craig stayed Richard's words. He pulled out a chair next to Trina and sat. "Do you want me to go back with you?"

The two answered in tandem. Richard with a firm 'yes', Trina with, "No. That is not necessary, Craig, though appreciated. We need to create a new normal for ourselves."

Trina turned to Richard. "We will discuss moving here in more detail and if it is what the family wants, we'll figure out the specifics later. Now, get your things packed so we can head out before it gets too late, we've got a long trip ahead of us as it is."

"Yes, ma'am," Richard muttered, and stomped into the room he shared with his brother.

Trina rubbed her throbbing temples. "Did you know Mike told him? When?"

"The day he considered running away."

"Guess I should've told him."

"No, Trina. You don't have to explain yourself or your past to your children. What Richard needs now is understanding and compassion, yes, but discipline and a sense of responsibility, as well. He wants to protect you and his younger siblings but at fourteen, there's only so much he can do. It frustrates him. And I'm sure it frightens him a bit too. I don't mind going back with you today, or I can leave tomorrow, if that'll help you, and Richard, feel a bit safer. I know I'd feel better."

"So would I." Lexie joined in on the conversation. She'd settled in a chair beside Trina and rubbed her well-rounded abdomen. "I wish Ace and I could go with y'all, but he's got too much going on right now with his internship and helping out on the ranch. We can't help but worry, Mom."

Trina hugged her daughter. "I understand. Let's just wait and see what happens. As long as Jack is in the hospital or jail, we're safe. I promise, the minute I hear something otherwise, I'll call." She turned to Craig. "You can be there in a day, so if you hear before me, just head on over. Head over any time you want, of course, but I'd like at least a week or so alone with my children to figure out what's next for us as a family."

Craig acknowledged her request with a nod of acquiescence. "Agreed."

Chapter Nine

The weeks flew, or dragged by, depending on the day, the hour, and person involved. Ace finished his final semester of veterinarian medicine and completed his internship at a local animal hospital. Craig got back in the swing of running his ranch. Lexie wavered between joy and sadness as grief too often eclipsed the excitement of the impending birth of her and Ace's son. Phone calls to and from Louisiana were the highlight of everyone's day.

Nearly ninety days after the altercation, Jack Simmons was taken directly from the hospital to the Lafayette Parish Jail, where he was denied bail due to his violent past with Katrina as well as Scott's death.

Katrina folded their last load of laundry and had barely put it away when the boys got home from school. Although she normally dropped them off and picked them up, she'd agreed to let the two walk with their friends these last few days. She heard the group whooping and hollering as they entered the garage.

"Hey, Mom, can the gang come in for snacks?"

Trina brushed the hair off Robert's forehead. "Sure. As long as it's all right with the parents."

Mild chaos ensued as each boy called his mother or father for permission to stay a while. Soon they were all settled around the kitchen table and snack bar laughing, joking and eating. Trina escaped into the den with Rikki. The two were on the floor playing when the doorbell rang.

"I'll get it," Richard yelled.

"No, Richard, wait..." But she was too late. He opened the door before she could stop him. Luckily, Mike graced their stoop.

"Hey." The two males high-fived.

"Hope you don't mind me dropping by unannounced."

"Not at all. We've got a kitchen full of boys, but

you're welcome to join us. At your own risk," Trina said with a laugh.

Mike chuckled and followed them in. He visited with the boys a few minutes then joined Trina and Rikki in the den. "Whew! And I thought the ER was noisy." Rikki rushed over with a squeal and he bent to pick her up. "Hey, Princess."

"Hey, Mi'ter Mike."

"What'cha doing?"

"Me building a castle wif Mommy."

"Ahh, so I see."

She wriggled from his embrace and pulled him by the hand to sit beside Trina on the floor.

"So, when are y'all heading out to Bandera?"

"Oh, a day or two. Lexie's not due for another couple of weeks. She's begun effacing but no dilation yet." She blinked rapidly and swallowed hard.

Mike ran a hand down her arm. "What?"

Trina brushed at the moisture on her cheeks. "She

wanted Scott to deliver the baby."

Mike cocooned her against his side and pressed her face into his shoulder. "Yeah. He was pretty excited about that. Do you think she'd want me to do it?"

Trina allowed his comfort for a moment then eased away. "I think she's got everything scheduled with her regular doctor. But thank you for offering."

They sat in silence a few minutes then Rikki demanded to go potty. Trina scrambled up to help her daughter and Mike returned to the kitchen to visit with the kids.

Soon the neighboring children wandered home and Trina prepared a light dinner, inviting Mike to stay.

They'd barely finished eating when the phone rang. Trina answered. "Hello?"

"Hey, it's Craig. How's everything and everyone?"

"We're fine. Just finished supper. Is everything okay over there? Lexie's not in labor, is she?"

"No, no, she's fine. I wanted...." His voice cracked;

words trailed off. He cleared his throat. "I wonder if you could bring the letter with you?"

"Letter?"

"Yeah. Scott said you knew where his mother's letter was, and if anything were to happen to him, you'd give it to me."

"Sure. I'll bring it. Anything else?"

"Have y'all decided on living arrangements yet?"

"No. We really haven't discussed it to any degree. I'm sure we'll make some decisions over the summer."

"Okay. Guess we'll see y'all in a few days."

"Yep."

"Good deal. Well, hug the kids for us. Let me know when you're on your way and keep us posted on the trip."

"Will do." Trina smiled as she hung up the phone.

"Decisions about what? If you don't mind my asking."

Trina poured Mike and herself each a mug of coffee

and joined him at the table. "Richard initially didn't want to return here after Easter and Spring Break. He even mentioned us moving to Bandera...."

Her words trailed off at the shocked disbelief on his face.

"You're not honestly thinking about a permanent move, are you?"

"I don't know what I'm considering. At this point, I'm lucky to make it through an entire day without falling apart. Our lives are a mess and the situation with Jack does not make it easier. Speaking of which, I wish you'd never mentioned that to my fourteen-year-old son."

A dark flush climbed into his cheeks. Mike shifted his gaze from hers and mumbled an apology.

"Isn't there a law or something about sharing private information?"

Mike nodded. "Yeah, and you could make sure I never practice medicine again if you want. Although I hope you don't choose to take that route. Craig and I both thought the boy needed a wake-up call. Maybe it was the wrong approach, but you'd been through so much already and Richard wasn't helping."

"He's right, Mom, so don't blame him or Uncle Craig."

Both turned to find Richard in the kitchen doorway.

"Sorry, I didn't mean to eavesdrop, just wanted to grab some water."

"Go ahead and get some then," Trina said.

Richard walked to the refrigerator and retrieved a bottle of water then turned to face her. "Please don't get him into trouble. I needed to know so I can help protect you, Robert and Rikki Jayne."

"It's not your place to protect us. It's mine to protect my children."

"Like it or not, I'm the man of the house now, Mom, and I'll do my best to make Dad proud of me."

"So as man of the house, you think we should move

to Bandera?"

"I think we should discuss it."

Trina's eyes widened at the maturity in her son's answer, especially after years of adolescent belligerence. "We will, then. Later."

"Ok. See you later, Mike."

Trina shot her son a stern glance. "Uh, being man of the house does not give you the privilege of calling your elders by their first name. It's disrespectful."

"Sorry. No disrespect intended, Mr. Mike."

"Thank you, Richard, none taken."

An awkward silence sprang up between them. Mike cleared his throat and touched Trina's hand. "I know you've got a lot going on and you want to make the right choices, those in the best interest of your children, but please think long and hard before pulling up stakes and moving."

Again, Trina allowed his comfort momentarily, then

pulled away. "I will."

"You know I'm here for you, anytime, day or night."

Trina nodded. "Yes, but you have to work. I know a doctor's schedule firsthand and even if you lived closer, you can't be here all the time. It's obvious Jack's sick...."

"Jack is an addict," Mike interjected, cutting off her words.

"Right. Addicted. To what besides alcohol?"

"There were all sorts of drugs in his toxic screening as well as lethal doses of alcohol. I'm surprised he lived through detox. Probably have been better off had he not. He's got a long road ahead of him."

"Have you any idea what the procedure is?"

"Well, we do know he's been denied bail. I guess it's a matter of time before he goes to trial."

Trina's hand trembled when she lifted the now-cold coffee to her lips. "Unless some public defender gets him off."

"I doubt that, not with Scott's death in the equation.

He may get some charges reduced but Jack will more than likely spend quite a few years in jail."

"Yeah, and it's the 'more than likely' part that scares me. There's no guarantee of anything. In the ten years we were married, I saw Jack get out of so many scrapes it was ridiculous."

"And that's why you're so afraid."

"The biggest reason," Trina admitted. "But I also.... I don't know if I can stand being in this house without Scott."

The ache in her voice slashed at his composure. Mike resisted the urge to pull her into his arms and promise to protect her and the kids just as Scott would have. *Way too soon for that.* "I understand, but promise you'll call if you need or want to talk, or if I can do anything—anything at all—for you or the kids. You're like family to me and I love you all."

"I promise."

They chatted for a while before Mike left with

obvious reluctance. Trina settled her children in for the night. Afterward, she climbed into the bed she'd shared with her husband, wrapped his pillow in her arms, and cried herself to sleep.

Chapter Ten

Michael Charles Guidry paced the floor of his small apartment, which was located close to the hospital where he'd worked alongside Scott for years. His memory rolled back through the decades... the moment he and Scott first collided in the ER... when Scott met Katrina... the birth of their children... Images flooded his mind and filled his eyes with bittersweet tears. He slumped into a chair, folded his arms on the table, buried his face in them and let the floodgates open. Spent, he questioned his sanity at being in love with his best friend's wife.

For years he'd denied his feelings for Katrina and went on about his life. He'd been in and out of relationships, endured a failed marriage, and tried every trick known to man to avoid obsessing over the one woman who made his heart skip a thud every time he saw her. He'd never admitted this fact to anyone, not even himself, before now. He loved and respected Scott too much. Even now, the thought almost made him cringe.

Almost.

The idea of her moving to Texas scared the hell out of him, and the possibility of her developing feelings for Craig Harris terrified him even more. Surely, she wouldn't fall for Scott's *brother*.

Mike knew the story of how the two men were raised as neighbors but even someone who didn't deal in Medicine, in Biology and Science, could look at them and know they were related. He also knew the letter Trina had taken to Craig answered the questions as to their parentage.

He pushed himself out of the chair, strode into the kitchen, and opened a beer. His phone vibrated as he popped the top. Mike hesitated in taking it out of his pocket and said a quick, fervent prayer that Trina would finally call. He hadn't talked to her since she and the kids reported their safe arrival in Bandera six days ago. *But who's counting?*

Lexie's bound to have had that baby by now.

When the pulsating stopped, Mike checked his missed call list. No number he recognized. He waited a beat then listened to the voicemail. *Damn solicitors.*

He blocked the number, flipped the volume on, and nearly dropped the device when it rang again. Trina's name and number flashed on the screen. Mike hit the answer icon. "Hey, I was just thinking about you all."

"It's a boy! He looks just like Ace, except his hair is more red than blonde." She laughed, clearly excited, then burst into sob. "He looks like Scott, like my sons did when they were born. Oh, I'm sorry, I should be happy, not babbling like a fool. My emotions are all over the place right now."

"That's OK. I'm glad you called. You have no need to apologize to me, Trina. Ever. For anything."

"They're naming him Adam Craig Harris the Fifth."

Mike chuckled. "That's a mouthful. What will they call him?"

Trina laughed, as he hoped she would. "I guess since William has outgrown the nickname Bucko, he'll inherit it, or Buckaroo or something. No idea, really. Not even sure the kids have decided. Everyone is ecstatic..." Her words trailed off as minor chaos erupted around her.

Mike held the phone away from his ear and winced. "Send me pics."

"I will."

"Take care and let's talk soon."

She hung up and he had no idea if she heard his parting remarks. His phone pinged...and then again and again as picture after picture arrived, complete with funny captions and hilarious anecdotes, of the newest member of the Hensley/Harris clan. The sheer magnetism of Trina's joy sent an ache to his soul.

What am I supposed to do, Lord? Scott, can you

hear me? I swear I'll love, honor, and cherish her as no one, other than you, ever could.

The next morning Mike awoke from one of the clearest, sweetest, most realistic dreams he'd had in...well, decades. Taking it as a sign from God and Scott, he placed a call, made lodging reservations, and packed a suitcase. His vacation started in two days and for once in his long career as a physician, he would not be accessible to get called in for an emergency or to shorten his time off.

* * *

Mike drove up to the Hensley House B&B in Bandera, Texas, and checked his messages before unloading his luggage. He loved Bandera, often wondered how anyone who grew up here could move away but understood Scott's need to do so after the death of his parents and first wife nearly thirty years ago.

Inside and unpacked, he reclined on the king-size

bed and let the peace and quiet envelop him.

Be a great place to set up a practice. Or retire.

Though technically too young to retire, the idea of settling here held a certain appeal. Oh, he had enough money to retire, just wasn't old enough.

"Enough of that, man," he chided himself aloud and lunged from the bed to pace. "If you don't, win her heart, in due time, you may be hauling butt in a totally opposite direction with your tail tucked between your legs."

The pound of feet and blended voices echoed from the stairs leading to the fourth floor of the home. *The Family Suite.*

This wasn't the first time he'd visited Bandera with the Hensley family. Therefore, Mike knew the entire top floor of the B&B consisted of a two-bedroom apartment where Scott, Trina, and the children usually stayed when they visited for any length of time. They used to bed down with Craig and his bunch, but as both families continued to grow, more room became necessary to house the lot of them.

He went into the bathroom and freshened up, then changed his shirt. He hesitated in front of the mirror, pleased at the reflection staring back at him.

At fifty, his physique held only minor traces of fat, thanks to good genes as well as solid eating and exercise habits. His sandy-colored hair sported a few silver streaks. Laugh lines added character to hazel eyes. A dimple creased his right cheek. *All in all, looking pretty good, old man.* And a hell'uva lot closer to Trina's age than Craig—or even Scott for that matter. He cringed at the ungraciousness of the thought and sent up a silent plea for forgiveness. Sitting on the edge of the bed, he tried to pray. "God, if this is even remotely Your will, let them receive me joyfully this evening."

Mustering his courage, Mike climbed the stairs to the next floor. Before he could chicken out, he knocked.

Trina opened the door and he'd have given every

ounce of gold he had to capture the surprised pleasure on her face in a photograph.

"Hey! Why didn't you tell us you were coming?"

"Wanted to surprise you all. Hey, boys," he greeted as Richard and Robert appeared at their mother's side.

"Mi'ter Mike, Mi'ter Mike!" Rikki's exuberant greeting struck him in the heart as she flung herself in his arms.

"Hey, Princess."

"Wexie gotta new baby."

"So, I hear. You like him?"

Red-gold curls bounced off her shoulders when she nodded. "I wanna take him home." Her little lips puckered. "But Mommy says we can't."

Mike chuckled. "That wouldn't be very fair to Tamera Joy, now would it, to take her baby brother?"

A pout creased her pert lips and furrowed her tiny brow. "Not fair." She turned to her mother. "I wanna baby brother."

Trina laughed. "I don't think that's going to happen. Besides, you already have two brothers."

Her smile could have melted a glacier. "Yeah, but I wanna baby."

Laughter resonated throughout the hallway at her insistence. Trina reached for her, but she clung to Mike.

"We're about to head over to the ranch for dinner. You're welcome to join us. The whole crew will be there."

"You sure Craig and them won't mind? I don't want to invite myself."

She smiled. "You're not. I'm inviting you. They'll love to see you and you know it. Scott had mentioned earlier this year that you might join us after the baby's birth."

"Yeah, we'd talked about it, before...." His voice broke. He swallowed hard. "But I wasn't sure whether the information had reached Craig or not."

"Doesn't matter." Trina scoffed, blinking furiously.

How often did she need to curb those tears? "You can ride with us. C'mon, kids, let's go."

He smiled and flicked a tear off her cheek with his thumb. "As you wish, ma'am."

Mike strapped Rikki into her car seat while the boys climbed in and hooked up their safety belts. Then he opened the front passenger door, climbed in beside Trina, and buckled up.

Trina glanced in the rearview mirror. "Everybody ready?"

The answer was a chorus of "yes, ma'ams."

Mike turned to address the boys. "You guys been riding yet?"

"A little," Richard said.

"Yeah, couldn't go much, waiting on the little buckaroo to get here," Robert chimed.

"Guess he's found his nickname," Mike remarked with a laugh.

"Don't see why they can't just call him Little Ace or

something instead of that."

"Richard..." Trina's voice held a warning.

"Well, it's dumb. William being stuck with Bucko was bad enough."

"I'm sure Lexie will see to it her son has the nickname that suits him, and her, best," Mike interjected, hoping to soothe the tension escalating between Trina and her eldest. *He'll be my biggest challenge.* He eyed Richard out of his peripheral view. Their gazes met, held. Mike arched a determined brow at the young man. Richard narrowed his eyes then grinned as though he knew exactly why Mike was there.

Boy's not dumb.

"No, he's not, and he likes you." Relief eased the guilt in Mike's mind at Scott's whisper. His heart lifted. *Thanks, buddy.*

From the moment they turned into the Rockin' H drive, a cloud of dust preceded them all the way to the house. They disembarked from Trina's truck as Amber,

Stanley and their children piled out of theirs.

Hugs, handshakes, and warm welcomes relieved Mike of any lingering trace of fear that he was intruding on a family affair.

Everyone gathered around the crib and took turns 'oohing' and 'aahing' over the baby. Before long, the children's interest wandered from the little guy on to the more pressing matter of a game of horseshoes.

Mike extended his arms toward the crib. "May I?"

Lexie beamed. "Of course."

Mike lifted the infant into the cradle of his arms. "Such a handsome little lad," he cooed and wished fervently for a child of his own. Both his and Trina's ages would prevent them from ever having one. He heard Craig say his name in a questioning tone and shifted his thoughts back into the present moment. "I'm sorry, what?"

"You okay there? Seemed a little out of it for a moment."

Mike emitted a self-conscious little laugh. "Yeah, mind went off on a tangent. Always does when I'm holding a newborn. Nothing more precious."

"Never had any of your own, did you?"

"No. Wish I had, but no," he said, his tone wistful. "Maybe one day though, I'll find the right woman, settle down and perhaps adopt."

Curiosity lifted Craig's brow. "Unless she already has children."

Mike avoided full eye contact with Craig unease creeping through his system at the insinuation in Craig's voice. Did Craig have any idea how he felt about Trina? Was he that transparent? He shrugged. "Cross that bridge when I get to it."

Rikki tugged on his pant leg, offering a welcomed diversion. Mike cuddled her close as the little girl crawled into his lap, demanding she hold the baby. He adjusted Little Ace so that she could get her arms around him.

"Sweet widdle Ace," she whispered, kissing and cooing until Tamera scrambled over to protest.

"My baby," she insisted, doing her best to get in Mike's lap also.

Laughing, Craig came to his rescue. "Hang on, Tamera. PaPaw will help you hold him in a minute. Mister Mike's lap's not big enough for all of you."

Before they could make the switch, the baby began to squirm and fuss.

Lexie lifted him from Mike's embrace. "I'll just take him inside to nurse and change and we'll be right back out.

The evening passed without further incident. Everyone left well after dark to return to their various lodgings. Mike herded the grumpy boys to their room while Trina changed Rikki and tucked her into bed. She joined him in the kitchen for a mug of tea.

"Lovely evening. You've got a beautiful grandson there, Ms. Hensley."

"To quote William, '*yep, my do.*'"

Her smile took his breath away. Mike hesitated in touching her and pushed back from the table. "Guess I'll see you all in the morning."

Trina rose and escorted him to the door. "Guess so."

"You need anything at all, I'm right downstairs."

"Thanks, Mike. Sleep well."

* * *

Craig lingered on the porch long after everyone had cleared out. He welcomed Ace and accepted the glass of Scotch his son handed him with a smile and silent salute.

"What'cha thinking, Dad?"

Craig shrugged, sipped. "Nothing really, just enjoying the quiet of the evening."

"Hard won at that," Ace said with a laugh.

Craig chuckled. "Lexie and the kids sleeping?"

"Tamera's having a bit of trouble settling down. Lex

is reading to her. I offered, but she wants her mama."

"Little bit of jealousy there. She'll get over it."

"Yeah. Been quite a day. She's pretty worn out, just doesn't want to give in."

Conversation waned into companionable silence.

"Kinda surprised when Mike showed up with Trina and the boys."

Ace shifted in his chair. "I was too, but Lexie said Trina mentioned that he and Scott had talked about him coming up on vacation while they were here. Does it bother you, though, him being around with Scott gone?"

"He's a good man and has been a wonderful friend to them for a long time."

Ace raised his tumbler to his lips, paused, then tossed back the last of his drink. "That's not what I'm asking."

Craig leaned forward and placed his empty shot glass on the porch rail. "Spit it out, Ace."

"Does it bother you that he's around Trina?"

"Why would it bother me?"

"Well, if you think you're developing feelings for her...."

"It's way too soon for that." Craig cut off his son's words. "Besides, she's my brother's wife."

Ace picked up his father's jigger and stood. "Your brother's widow and I'm not insinuating anything wrong here, Daddy. But if you think you'd want her to be more than that to you in the future, I want you to know it's OK to let it happen."

Craig buried his face in his palms as Ace went back into the house. He'd promised Scott he'd take care of Trina and the kids should anything happen to him but had no idea he'd be called upon to do so less than five years after making the vow. The age difference between Scott and Trina hadn't bothered Scott, but at damn near sixty-three, Craig never thought he'd even be considering raising children.

Dear God, was that what Scott meant when he asked me to look after them?

Chapter Eleven

Ace's comments incited a whole slew of questions for Craig. *How* did *he feel about Trina? Could he love her as a husband? What would that mean to the rest of his family?*

For the next few days, he observed more, talked less. He opened his heart and mind, tried to imagine her in his arms. In his bed. Living with her and the children, day after day. Very pleasant meanderings but he couldn't seem to reconcile himself to the idea of another wife much less raising another man's children. Even his brother's.

When Mike's vacation neared its end, Craig sat with him, Trina and Richard discussing the possibility of the Hensley family moving to Bandera permanently.

"I think we should." Richard remained adamant in his desire to relocate.

Mike didn't seem to want them to do so. "But what

about school and your and Robert's friends? You've been going to the same school with mostly the same people your entire life."

"None of that matters. All that matters is making sure Mama and my brother and sister are safe. We can always make new friends."

Trina reached over and ran a hand through her son's hair. "This is a big decision, Richard, and we don't need to make it out of sheer emotion. Moving would take a whole lot of time and work. We've got years of life to sort through. Why don't we go home at the end of summer and see how things go? As far as we know, Jack will not be getting out of jail anytime soon, so we have some time."

"That's just it, Mom, we don't *know* if or when he will get out and what if we don't find out until it's too late and he shows up at our house or at school?"

"Would you feel better if I found a place closer or Craig spent more time with you all?" Mike turned to

Craig. "You could do that, couldn't you?"

Craig nodded. "Be glad to. As often and as long as necessary for Richard to feel safe and confident."

Richard's jaw muscle twitched. "I thought you were serious when you said we would discuss moving. Now y'all are just ignoring what I want and ganging up on me, so I'll give in to what *you* think is best!"

The boy lunged from his chair. Mike stood and halted his escape. "That's not the case at all, Richard. We understand your fears and concerns. Believe me, we have them too. We just have more life experience and know this is not an easy or quick solution. By the time your mom would get everything in order, the situation with Jack will probably be resolved. Chances are, he won't see the light of day outside a jail or prison facility for a long time."

Richard heaved an agitated breath. "It's the slim chance he will get off that scares me. Besides, people escape all the time." His eyes filled; lip trembled. His gaze sought Trina's. "I don't want to lose you too."

Trina pushed back from her seat and embraced him. "I promise we will be vigilant. Craig will come as often and stay as long as he can. I am not ignoring your wishes. In fact, I think moving is not such a far-fetched idea. I've considered your feelings and my own about staying in that house without your father and it's not going to be easy, no matter what we decide. But we also have to consider Robert's view on the idea and the little I've talked with him, he doesn't want to move."

"What if I talk to him?"

Trina shook her head. "I don't want him to know what you know, Richard. He's too young and I don't want him frightened unnecessarily. Let's keep the discussion open and pray for wisdom and direction." She switched her gaze to the men. "How soon could the B&B be dismantled and returned to just a home? Would that even be possible?"

"Anything is possible if that's what you want to do,"

Craig assured.

"Either way, I'll start looking for a place closer to y'all as soon as I get home," Mike promised.

* * *

As it turned out, none of their fears materialized. Two days later, Trina received a call from her lawyer informing her Jack had died. She hung up the phone and asked the wrangler at the Hensley House B&B to saddle a horse for her, then took a long ride where she allowed the emotions roiling within her soul to run their course—pain, anger, relief and finally, sadness. She prayed for Jack's soul and that she and her children would come through this valley stronger and closer. She still had no idea if she could keep living in their huge house—which seemed so empty—without Scott.

The jangle of her cell phone startled her out of her reverie. Mike's name flashed on the screen. He'd left for Louisiana early that morning.

"Hey, you made it home already?"

"Yep. Just pulled into the drive. Haven't even unloaded my suitcase yet."

"Glad you're safe."

"I miss you guys already."

She laughed. "We'll see you in a few weeks."

"Hopefully, I'll have found a house or another apartment by then."

"No need. Jack died yesterday. My attorney called a while ago."

"Oh. How do you feel after hearing the news?"

Trina swallowed the lump of emotion clogging her airwaves. "A myriad of emotions, relief being the uppermost, and guilt for feeling that."

"You have no reason to feel guilty. The man put you through hell for too long."

"True. Doesn't mean I wanted him dead though."

"I know, Trina. Neither did I. But I can't pretend I'm not relieved at the thought of you and the kids being safe from him. You didn't see him that night, but I'll never forget it. Have you told Richard yet?"

"No. I'll tell him when I get back and when Ace drops them off from their trip to town."

"Where are you?"

"Out on a ride."

"Alone?"

"Yes. I've been out here before and the ranch hands know where I am."

"Ok. Just be careful and safe...and call when you get a chance."

"Will do. I'll let the family know you're home too."

"Thanks."

She disconnected the call, mounted her horse, and entered the corral just as the boys returned with Ace. The housekeeper stepped out of the kitchen carrying Rikki who'd been down for a nap when Trina left for her ride.

Rikki's squeal of delight pierced the air. "Mama, horse!"

Trina laughed. She lifted her daughter out of Rosalie's arms and placed her in the saddle, then held her firmly while Ace led the horse around the paddock. Richard paced alongside them opposite of Trina and helped hold his sister in place while Robert walked next to her, jabbering about where they'd been and what they'd done.

Ace chuckled. "Give your mom a chance to catch a breath, Robert. Y'all coming for dinner tonight as planned?"

"I think we'll stay in tonight. Have a quiet evening."

Her statement met with protests from both boys as well as Ace. "If you need some time alone, I can take the kids home with me."

"I doubt Lexie is up to taking care of these three along with your two."

Ace grinned. "She won't be taking care of them by herself. Who knows, Daddy might escape and crash your quiet evening to get some peace himself."

"That's Ok. Let me freshen up and we'll see y'all in a while."

Ace handed the reins to the wrangler and kissed Trina on the cheek before leaving for the Rockin' H. Trina had to wrestle Rikki a bit to get her out of the saddle but soon the entire family was cleaned up and ready to follow in his wake.

Over dessert and coffee, Trina told Craig, Ace, Lexie, and Richard the news about Jack and that Mike had made it home safe.

Chapter Twelve

The weeks passed quickly as time usually does when there's fun to be had. Upon hearing of Jack's death, Richard wasn't so adamant about moving, although he agreed with his mother that the house was too big and empty without his daddy. The family had barely arrived home and settled into a routine when hurricane warnings and watches put them on alert for evacuation. Although they weren't directly in the path of the storm, Craig convinced Katrina to bring the kids to Bandera when the hurricane bearing her name swept the Louisiana/Mississippi coast east of Lafayette. They stayed through Labor Day and returned home, only to turn around and leave again less than a month later due to Hurricane Rita which made landfall west of them.

"Whew! If two hurricanes back-to-back isn't a sign you should move here, I don't know what is," Lexie beseeched her mother.

"You might have a point," Trina admitted, tucking Rikki into her bed at the Hensley House. Her phone rang.

"Hello?"

"Y'all made it safe?" Mike asked.

"Yes. I've just put Rikki to bed. The boys are settled, and Lexie is here. How are you?"

"Done. As soon as this crap is over, I'm done. Made up my mind a while ago. I want a less stressful place to practice medicine."

"Any idea where that might be?"

"Anywhere you and the kids are."

"Oh..." Trina's cheeks grew warm. "Well...we'll have to make a decision about that soon, I guess. Meanwhile, you take care. Talk to you later," she said and disconnected the call before he could say another word.

"Was that Mike?"

Trina nodded. Her cheeks still smarted.

"Why are you all flustered? What did he say?"

Trina sank onto the bed and raised a wary gaze to her daughter. "He said he's done there. Wants a less stressful place to practice medicine."

Lexie frowned. "So, what about that has you upset?"

"He wants to be wherever the kids and I are."

A smile bloomed on Lexie's face. Her brilliant green gaze danced. "That's wonderful."

"No, Lex, it's not. It's too soon. Scott's only been gone six months."

Lexie sat beside Trina, wrapped an arm around her and hugged her close. "There's no law of morality or etiquette that says how long you have to be alone after your spouse dies. Your vows say until death do you part. Not death and a year. Not even death and a day. Do you care about Mike?"

"Of course, I care. I've known him for more than a decade. He's a great guy."

"Then what's the problem?"

"I've never really been alone. I met Scott while still

married to Jack and although we lived separately and took our time dating, we were still in a relationship. I'm just not sure I'm ready for another so soon."

"Then don't rush into one. I'm sure Mike understands. He loved Scott too. But, Mom, you know Scott wouldn't want you to mourn forever."

Trina blew out a breath. "This is all too much to take in right now. He's probably just frustrated at the chaos over there with the hurricanes. Who knows how he'll feel tomorrow."

Lexie giggled and kissed Trina's cheek. "Yeah, you hold on to that belief as long as you can."

Trina heard her chuckle all the way out the door.

* * *

December 31, 2005

Craig sat on the porch alone. Scott's mother's letter lay, unopened, on his lap. Many times, he'd started to read it, but something always stopped him. Intuition or the soft restraint of the Holy Spirit, he didn't know, but he'd always put the document away.

Until now.

On the cusp of a new year, he figured now was as good a time as any.

Lifting the envelope, he slid his finger under the flap and removed the thin parchment stationary.

My darling son, your father has encouraged me for years to write this letter. The words contained within these pages may bring you anger and pain, perhaps bitterness or shame. Read them anyway and read them often, keeping in mind how very much you are loved and that your life, your very existence—no matter how painful—is worth far more than words can express. It is my prayer that you will end up with a deeper realization and understanding of the healing power of love and the saving grace of our Lord Jesus Christ.

Your father and I were married two short months when we discovered that we could never have a child of our flesh. Still, we trusted God to send us the perfect son or daughter at His will. Imagine our surprise when my cousin Helena Maria Hernandez showed up on our doorstep, pregnant and distraught. Her family disowned her for conceiving out of wedlock and wanted us to take her on the missionary trip your father was scheduled to undertake.

We never hesitated, but conditions were made. I never really knew the truth of whether or not Adam Harris, your biological father, compromised Helena by force. She didn't disclose that information but, as she was wild and irresponsible at the time, I would dare to say their encounter was consensual....

Craig's fingers tightened on the paper; knuckles whitened. He took a deep breath, willed his hands not to shake and forcefully restrained from ripping the pages to shreds. Would his father, even as no good as he

was, force himself on a woman? *God, I hope not.*
Regardless, how many other illegitimate children were
out there? When would they come crawling out of
obscurity to claim part of what he'd worked so hard to
build after his father left everything in ruins? He made
a mental note to speak with his attorney then continued
reading....

*Anyway, after much thought, prayer and
petitions, she agreed to give her child to us to raise as
our own since we could provide the kind of life for you,
she never could as a young, impetuous girl with no
training or skills.*

*Thankfully, by the time we were settled back in
Bandera, Helena had changed and became the woman
you knew her to be as the Harris's housekeeper, going
only by her Christian name, Maria.*

Craig stopped reading, stunned at the revelation.
The woman who had lived with his family from the time
he was five years old, who helped him grow into the

man he was and who'd loved and cherished him, his mother and grandfather, Tamera, and even Amber, had given birth to his brother?

Little memories began to surface, vignettes of the times Scott had visited, and the tender way Maria always behaved toward him. The tears she'd shed when she thought no one watched. The air of sadness that surrounded her from time to time, which lifted when she spent time with 'her boys' as she'd called them.

How had she lived in the same house as his father and nothing ever been said? Was his father *that* selfish and self-centered he hadn't recognized her? Or had Maria changed in more than personality from the impetuous, irresponsible girl who'd given birth to a child out of wedlock to the woman they knew in a few short years?

Makes no difference now. Taking a breath Craig wiped the moisture from his eyes and continued reading.

Based on the conditions of your conception and birth and the turmoil which haunted the Harrises for years, Mr. Harris Sr., your father, and I, as well as Helena, agreed you boys would be better off not knowing the whole story. Although we tried to avoid out-and-out lies, we did our best to answer your questions with as much truth as possible and yet, maintain your status quo.

Hopefully, by the time you read this, I'll have had a lifetime to reassure you of the deep love your father and I have for you. We are so very proud of the man you've become, Scott, despite your choice to be a physician instead of a minister like your father (smile). Seriously, you have blessed our lives more than I can ever begin to express with mere words. I pray you can forgive a prideful, fearful woman for withholding the entire truth from you and that you'll continue to live a meaningful, honorable, and prosperous life.

Your loving mother.

Craig stared a long time at Rosa Sanchez Hensley's signature, imagining how Scott must have felt. They'd lived a lifetime as best friends cognizant of the fact they could very well be brothers. Yet they never allowed the rumors or speculations to taint the bond they shared. *I'd love to talk to you now. Know how you feel.*

As though in answer to his silent plea, a breeze ruffled the papers on his lap and a tiny slip of paper slid from between the pages. How had he not noticed?

Craig shrugged and unfolded the note, Scott's penmanship, undeniable...

Hey, brother. If you're reading this, I'm no longer with you in the flesh but my spirit lives on, in your heart and in our memories. I know you'll receive this information with grace and humility just as I did, and not let any of the facts tarnish who you—who we—are, who you thought you were, or the man you've become. Guess we always knew though, right?

Doesn't matter, your love and friendship have blessed me from the first time we met until the day I left this earth. I thank you for your promise to look after Trina and my children. Whether or not your and Trina's feelings grow into that of more than loving friends and in-laws, I know you'll see to it they want for nothing. Although, unless I'm mistaken, Mike may give you a bit of competition. Which is fine too. I trust him as much as I do you.

Either way, no matter her choice in a future husband or staying unwed, I trust you to ensure they are always safe. Anyway, just wanted to leave this little reminder for you to rest assured, I am with you always... Scott.

websites where readers gather and/or your social media platforms (FaceBook, Good Reads, BookBub, Twitter, etc).

As always, it is my prayer that if you don't know Him, you will seek Jesus as your Lord and Savior and if you do, you'll endeavor to understand Him on a deeper, more personal level. And as always, may God bless and keep each and every one of you—and yours—in the palm of His loving hand.

Pamela S Thibodeaux
Inspirational with an Edge! ™
http://pamelathibodeaux.com

About the Author

Pamela S. Thibodeaux grew up in the town of Iowa, Louisiana. She is the mother of four (two by blood and two by marriage) and a grandmother. A deeply committed Christian, Pamela firmly believes in God and His promises.

"God is very real to me, and I feel people today need and want to hear more of His truths wherever they can glean them. People are hungry for practical (and real) Christian values, not some 'holier-than-thou' dictates which are impossible to believe and difficult to live up to," Pamela says.

"I do my best to encourage readers to develop a personal relationship with God. The deepest desire of my heart is to glorify God and to get His message of faith, trust, and forgiveness to a hurting world."

Email Pamela at: pthibo7@gmail.com

Visit her website: http://www.pamelathibodeaux.com

Or blog: http://pamswildroseblog.blogspot.com

Sign up to receive ***Pam's Newsletter*** (http://bit.ly/psthibnewsletter) and get a FREE short story!

Also: be sure to follow Pam on Social Media! FaceBook, Twitter @psthib, Amazon Author Page, Instagram, Pinterest, GoodReads, and BookBub.

Other Titles by Pamela S. Thibodeaux

My Heart Weeps

After thirty years married to the man of her dreams, Melena Rhyker is devastated by her husband's death. Relief comes in the form of an artist's retreat at the Crossed Penn ranch in Utopia, TX. She rediscovers a forgotten dream as her artistic talent flourishes into that of a gallery-worthy artist. Will she have the courage to follow the path she was destined to travel?

Garrett Saunders has been on the run most of his life. Abused and abandoned as a child, he escapes the clutches of a past filled with pain and shame, and hides from his calling as a Native American healer. His years as a CIA agent aid in overcoming his childhood and honing his talent and skill as a fine art photographer.

Follow their journey as two people who come from totally different backgrounds, but share gifts of gigantic proportions, find meaning and purpose in the Texas Hill Country.

Anytime is the perfect time for love.

In ***Love in Season***, author Pamela S Thibodeaux brings together eight of her most beloved romance stories—one for each season plus four holidays that revolve around love and family. Includes (Winter) Winter Madness, (Valentine's Day) Choices, (Spring) Cathy's Angel, (Easter) Lilies for Sandi (NEW!), (Summer) The Big Catch (NEW!), (Fall) A Hero for Jessica, (Thanksgiving) Review of Love (NEW!) and (Christmas) In His Sight.

Keri's Christmas Wish

For as long as she can remember, Keri Jackson has despised the hype and commercialism around Christmas so much she seldom enjoys the holiday. Will she get her wish and be free of the angst to truly enjoy Christmas this year?

A devout Christian at heart, Jeremy Hinton, a Psychotherapist, Life Coach, Spiritual Mentor and Energy Medicine Practitioner has studied all of the world's religions and homeopathic healing modalities. But when a rare bacterial infection threatens the life of the woman he loves, will all of his faith and training be for naught?

Set at the tail end of the Vietnam War era, ***Circles of Fate*** takes the reader from Fort Benning, Georgia to Thibodaux, Louisiana. A romantic saga, this gripping novel covers nearly twenty years in the lives of Shaunna Chatman and Todd Jameson. Constantly thrown together and torn apart by fate, the two are repeatedly forced to choose between love and duty, right and wrong, standing on faith or succumbing to the world's viewpoint on life, love, marriage and fidelity. With intriguing twists and turns, fate brings together a cast of characters whose lives will forever be entwined. Through it all is the hand of God as He works all things together for the good of those who love Him and are called according to His purpose.

Love is a Rose (devotional)

Music is the magical entry into the spirit world; the golden gate into the Kingdom of God. But we mustn't be of the mindset that God only uses Christian music to reach out and touch our mind, heart and spirit. God uses any and ***every*** means available to speak to His children.

Our job is to be open and receptive.

In this devotional, Pamela S Thibodeaux shares how God opened her spirit to a deeper understanding of the abundance of His grace and mercy through the words of the song, The Rose sung by Country & Western artist Conway Twitty.

Pamela offers Seeds to Ponder and a prayer as she parallels the love of God and the Christian life to each verse of the song.

Lori's Redemption

Lori Strickland (introduced in *Tempered Fire*) has always been known as her father's "wild child" with no desire to change until she meets ex-bull-rider-turned-preacher, Rafe Judson. Her attempts to change her wanton ways come to naught until she realizes redemption only comes with true repentance. Can she find redemption and win the heart of the cowboy preacher?

The Tempered Series Collection ~ Start at the beginning and follow these beloved characters throughout the years as love crosses the lines of age and strengthens the bonds of friendship. Contains: ***Tempered Hearts, Tempered Dreams,***

Tempered Fire, Tempered Joy, Lori's Redemption

The Visionary

A visionary is someone who sees into the future Taylor Forrestier sees into the past but only as it pertains to her work. Hailed by her peers as *"a visionary with an instinct for beauty and an eye for the unique"* Taylor is undoubtedly a brilliant architect and gifted designer. But she and twin brother Trevor, share more than a successful business. The two share a childhood wrought with lies and deceit and the kind of abuse that's disgustingly prevalent in today's society. Can the love of God and the awesome healing power of His grace and mercy free the twins from their past and open their hearts to the good plan and the future He has for their lives? Find out in **The Visionary** ~ Where the awesome power of God's love heals the most wounded of souls.

The Inheritance *is about the chance we all long for...the chance to start over.* Widowed at age thirty-nine and suffering from empty nest syndrome, Rebecca Sinclair is overshadowed by grief and loneliness. Her husband has been deceased for a year, her oldest child has moved to New York in pursuit of an acting career and her youngest child is attending college in France. Having spent over half of her life as a wife and mother, she has no idea what God has in store for her now. Will an unexpected inheritance in the wine country of New York bring meaning and purpose to her life and give her the courage to love again?

US Postal worker Raymond Jacobey has been in love with the little widow since he first set eyes on her. A wanderer searching for the ever-illusive soul mate, Ray has never stayed in one place too long. Raised by self-centered, high-power executives, he's longed for the idyllic life of residing in a cozy house in a small town with the love of his life. Will he gain the heart of the lovely widow or will he lose her to the wine country of New York? Find out in ***The Inheritance***

Tempered Hearts (book 1 in Tempered series)*:* Rancher Craig Harris and veterinarian Tamera Collins clash from the moment they meet. Innocence is pitted against arrogance as tempers rise and passions ignite to form a love as pure as the finest gold, fresh from the crucible and as strong as steel. Thrown together amid tragedy and unsated passion, Tamera and Craig share a strong attraction that neither accepts as the first stages of love. Torn between desire and dislike, they must make peace with their pasts and God in order to open up to the love blossoming between them. It is a love that nothing can destroy when they come to understand that **only when hearts are tempered, minds are opened and wills are softened can man discern the will of God for his life.**

Tempered Dreams (book 2 in Tempered Series)

Dr. Scott Hensley (introduced in Tempered Hearts) has built a wall around his heart since the death of his wife and parents. Katrina Simmons is recovering from scars inflicted on her as a battered wife. Can dreams be renewed and faith strengthened? Can they find joy and peace in God's love and in love for one another?

Tempered Fire (book 3 in Tempered Series)

Amber Harris is a good girl on the brink of womanhood. Stanley Morrison is a young man at the start of his life. For each other, they have always felt the fireworks that two people in love should feel. But the questions about his past, his pride, and Amber's father might be the end of what could be a strong relationship. As the two try to protect their budding romance, some unlikely but powerful forces conspire to keep them apart. Will they survive the wishes of everyone around them with their relationship intact?

Tempered Joy (book 4 in Tempered series).

All around rodeo cowboy and heir to the Rockin' H Ranch, Ace Harris is determined not to fall in love. He's only loved one woman in his life, his mother, and no one can even come close to filling her boots. Lexie Morgan thinks rodeo cowboys have rocks for brains and a death wish for a soul. A broken childhood and the death of her father and best friend leave her doubting and questioning God (despite her years of religious upbringing) and afraid of love. Can two young people who clash from the onset learn to trust in the healing power of God and find love and happiness amidst tragedy and grief?

Lilies for Sandi *Part of ***Love in Season*** collection of short stories*

Sandi and Brett did everything backwards. They got pregnant before the wedding and had a baby instead of a honeymoon. Since, Brett has resented the fact that his dreams of a football career have been cut short and wonders how long it'll take God to forgive him for his mistakes. Sandi has played second fiddle to Brett's dreams and desires to the point of not knowing herself any longer and fears her marriage will never be a true one because of their failures. Can two hearts broken by unfulfilled dreams find healing, wholeness and restoration?

The Big Catch *Part of **Love in Season** collection of short stories*

Karla and, the love of her life, Jeff, have uncovered some uncommon ground: The Great Outdoors. For the life of her, she does not understand his love of fishing and how he can spend so much time doing so. Will she come to love the sport as much as he or will his passion for a rod and reel tangle up their relationship?

Review of Love *Part of **Love in Season** collection of short stories*

Jason Stockwell has been commissioned to interview Kylie Erickson and to review her books. Only problem is, she won't give the time of day much less an interview to someone whose type of writing she deems not worthy of respect. Can they suspend their judgmental attitudes and find true love?

Cathy's Angel *Part of **Love in Season** collection of short stories*

Single mom Cathy Johnson is tired of running her life alone...what she needs is a well-trained angel to help out. Jared Savoy gave up the dream of having a family when he discovered he is sterile. Can a confirmed bachelor and the mother of four find love amid normal daily chaos?

Choices *Part of **Love in Season** collection of short stories*

Best-selling novelist and songwriter, Camie Rogers has penned numerous accounts of the secret love she holds in her heart. Country-Music Superstar Kip Allen has changed from the shy, humble boy, to the epitome of "star." Can the two rediscover each other after one night of his Home is Where the Heart is Tour?

A Hero for Jessica *Part of **Love in Season** collection of short stories*

Anthony Paul Seville is known as the 'most eligible bachelor' in New Orleans, possibly even the entire state of Louisiana, but finds himself alone—completely and explicitly alone. Jessica Aucoin is a writer on her way to fame and fortune, but is haunted by a man from her past. Will the "champion" lawyer and the author of romantic suspense find love written in their future?

Sienna has survived what most succumb to - the death of a spouse and child and has maintained her faith despite her troubles. William has never met anyone who actually lived out what they say they believe. Is it true love between the faithful optimist and broody pessimist or simply **Winter Madness**? *Part of **Love in Season** collection of short stories*

In His Sight *Part of **Love in Season** collection of short stories*

Grade-school teacher Carson Alexander has a gift— a gift that has driven a wedge between him and his family. Worse, it's put him at odds with God. Feeling alone and misunderstood, Carson views God's gift of prophecy as the worst kind of curse...that is until he meets Lorelei Conner, landscape artist extraordinaire, and perhaps the one person who may need Carson and his gift more than anyone ever has.

Lorelei Connor is a mother on the run. Her abusive ex-husband has followed her all over the country trying to steal their daughter. Distrusting of men and needing to keep on the move, she's surprised by her desire to remain close to Carson Alexander. Through her fear and hesitation, she must learn to rely on God to guide her—not an easy task when He's prompting her to trust a man. Can their relationship withstand the tragedy lurking on the horizon?

Thank You.....

I pray you've been blessed as I have by your purchase of this book. If you've enjoyed ***Tempered Truth***, please write a positive review and post it at online retailers (Amazon, B&N, Kobo, iBooks, etc.) and websites where readers gather and/or your social media platforms (FaceBook, Good Reads, BookBub, Twitter, etc).

Sign up to receive my ***Newsletter*** (http://bit.ly/psthibnewsletter) and get a FREE short story.

**Temperance
Publishing**